The Treasure Code

Milton Dank & Gloria Dank

The Treasure Code

Milton Dank & Gloria Dank

Delacorte Press/New York

Published by
Delacorte Press
1 Dag Hammarskjold Plaza
New York, N.Y. 10017

Manufactured in the United States of America

First printing

LIBRARY OF CONGRESS CATALOGING IN PUBLICATION DATA

Dank, Milton [date of birth]
The treasure code.
(A Galaxy Gang mystery)
Summary: Six junior high school friends embark on a
search for the dragon ring, a valuable treasure
buried somewhere in the city of Philadelphia
by a local author who has written a book
containing clues to the treasure's hiding place.
[1. Mystery and detective stories.   2. Buried treasure
—Fiction.   3. Philadelphia (Pa.)—Fiction]
I. Dank, Gloria.   II. Title.
PZ7.D228Tr   1985   [Fic]
ISBN 0-385-29370-4
Library of Congress Catalog Card Number: 84–15569

To Michael, Jenny,
Chris, and Katie Zosa

CLUES FROM *DRAGONSTONE* BY DR. JOYCE HENNING

Recently retired as a professor of medieval history at the University of Pennsylvania, Dr. Joyce Henning gives the clues that lead to a valuable ring in the shape of a dragon, studded with precious gems, which she has buried somewhere in or near Philadelphia.

Clue Number One

Start at the center;
The center of the city,
The center of the government,
Will point you where you want to go.

Clue Number Two

From the center
Go to the old center,
Then to the center of the old center and the
    meetinghouse,
Then to the center of the center and the center
    of the old center and the meetinghouse.
Go slowly—don't be fooled!

Clue Number Three

CGCBCDCBCDGABCG

NOTE THESE LETTERS WELL!

Clue Number Four

You cannot see the forest for the trees,
Eleven of them all in a row.

Clue Number Five

If our fifth President
Had stood in Thomas Jefferson's shoes,
Where would he be now?

Clue Number Six

All the roads to heaven are not on one map. Even
rich uncles such as I seek other ways. Travel
every path you will.

Clue Number Seven

17163034546267
12025395968828799
12040556974

Clue Number Eight

When the eye watches you from the sky
And night is all around,

Pace out from where the shadow starts
And dig there in the ground.
The number of paces is twice the hour, three
   times the depth in feet, and equal to the
   month. If you count to ten, you'll have named
   them all.

1

□ "We're all going to be very, very rich," Sphinx announced.

The other members of the Galaxy Gang laughed. They had heard Sphinx's get-rich-quick schemes before. Larry shook his head. "What is it this time—a cobalt mine in Fairmount Park?"

"Nothing involving manual labor," Sphinx replied. "See this little book?" He held up a thin paperback.

"Another one of your crazy ideas," Chessie said. There was a murmur of agreement and, ignoring Sphinx, they started talking about their classes. Sphinx, like his namesake, just sat and smiled a mysterious smile.

It was a crisp fall day after school, and the Galaxy Gang had gathered at Chessie's house for a snack. A year ago the six junior-high-school students had banded together out of friendship and mutual respect. Each one seemed to add something to the gang: a talent, a skill, even a sense of humor. It was fun, and by now they were almost a family.

Tilo, a slim Vietnamese boy, leaned over Sphinx's shoulder.

"What is it?" he asked, taking the book out of Sphinx's hands and flipping the pages curiously. "It doesn't even make any sense!"

"Of course it doesn't!" Sphinx said, snatching the book back. "It's a treasure hunt, that's why, and these are the clues. If they made any sense, they wouldn't be clues, would they?"

"Treasure hunt?" Chessie echoed.

"I like the sound of it," Bobbie said, "but what's it got to do with us?"

Sphinx leaned forward over the table. "Riches," he said hoarsely, "beyond your wildest imagination. A treasure trove just waiting to be found!"

"Yeah, right," Larry said. "Riches that exist only in Sphinx's overactive imagination."

"First, I think I'll leave school," Sphinx said. "When I'm rich, that is. I'll leave school and spend the rest of my life on a tropical island. Or better yet, I'll buy a plane and fly around the world."

"Sounds great," Diggy said. "So what were we talking about?" he asked the others. "Did I tell you what my English teacher said to me today?"

"Our parents won't be able to push us around anymore," Sphinx continued. "We'll be independently wealthy—all of us. Not you, squirt," he said to

Chessie's little brother, Frankie, who came running into the kitchen. "This has nothing to do with you."

"I don't care!" Frankie yelled. *"I don't care!"* He went over to the refrigerator and jerked open the door, then slammed it shut. The whole gang jumped. He grinned at his sister. "Nothin' to eat," he announced.

"Frankie," said Chessie, "get out."

"Okay, okay. You don't have to tell me twice." Frankie went over and stood next to Sphinx.

"No," Chessie said in a low voice to Bobbie, "I have to tell him five times."

"I've seen that picture before," Frankie said, pointing at the book. The cover showed a green and golden dragon guarding a pile of sparkling jewels. "Isn't that book called *Dragonstone?*"

Sphinx looked around the table. "Great," he said. "A mere infant knows more about this book than you guys do. Yeah, that's the one, Frankie. Now get lost."

"One of my friends brought it in to school today," the little boy said. "I think it looks like fun. He said we should try to solve the clues."

"Wonderful, wonderful," Sphinx said. "We'd better hurry. The eight-year-olds are breathing down our necks." He flipped through the pages.

"You gonna try it?" Frankie asked, his eyes growing wide.

"No," Sphinx said. "I think it's boring. What's so great about buried treasure anyway?"

"I could help," Frankie offered.

"Maybe with the astronomy clues," Sphinx replied. "Or the codes. How much math have you had, Frankie?"

" 'Rithmetic."

"Okay, if I get hung up on one of these codes, you'll be the first person I call. Chessie, can't you do something with him?"

"Frankie, if you don't get lost, I'm going to kill you," his sister said sharply.

"Okay, okay!" Frankie backed out of the room.

"Well, so far I've got Frankie really interested in the idea," Sphinx said. "What about the rest of you?"

"What's it about?" Larry asked, reaching for the book.

"It just came out," Sphinx said. "It's by a local author, published here in Philadelphia. This lady—Joyce Henning—had an heirloom which she buried someplace in or around the city. She wrote a book with clues to the hiding place. People are going crazy over it. I'm telling you, she'll make a fortune. And *we're* going to solve the clues and make a fortune ourselves!"

Larry read aloud from the book. "The treasure is called the dragon ring. It is an antique ring which has been in my family for generations. It is made of eighteen-carat gold in the shape of a dragon with a valuable diamond coiled in its tail. The dragon's eyes are emeralds, and its body is studded with sapphires." He gave a low whistle. "Not bad."

"It sounds beautiful," Chessie murmured.

"The ring is worth approximately seventy-five thousand dollars," Larry continued. *"Wow!"*

"And it'll be worth even more by the time it's found," Sphinx put in. "With all the hoopla over this book, and fortune hunters swarming all over Philadelphia, the value of that ring is going up all the time."

"How can she afford to give it away like that?" Diggy asked.

"Oh, she's rich," Sphinx said with a wave of his hand. "Old money. Not to mention the fact that she's going to rake in a lot more just from sales of this book."

Chessie grabbed *Dragonstone* out of Larry's hand. "Let me see." She pored over the book. "Hmmm. Listen to this. 'You cannot see the forest for the trees,/ Eleven of them all in a row.' What does that mean?"

Bobbie took the book next. " 'From the center/Go to the old center,/Then to the center of the old center . . .' Great. I'm confused already."

"It can't be very easy," Tilo said. He flipped through the pages, each with a few lines of writing or numbers. "You don't want a lot of people finding the treasure."

"For us it'll be easy," Sphinx said. "See what it says here in the beginning. 'These clues draw upon knowledge in math, music, astronomy, Philadelphia geography, and United States history.' We can split up the puzzles according to the fields we're best at. Then we'll get back together, look at all the clues, and *voilà*—the treasure!"

"It's not a bad idea," Diggy said, "but with thousands of people looking for—"

"Oh, c'mon, where's your sense of adventure?" Sphinx urged. "Don't be such a drag, Diggy. I just *know* we can find it."

"I think it's great," Chessie said, her eyes glowing. "Buried treasure!"

"That's the spirit," said Sphinx. "How about the rest of you?"

"I like it," Tilo said. "Why couldn't it be us? We're just as likely as anyone else to find it."

"Okay, I'm in," Larry said, laughing. " 'Who dares nothing, need hope for nothing.' Schiller, a German writer."

"I'll go along with it," said Robbie.

Diggy smiled. "It's not like one of our regular cases," he said, "but why not? I could use something to think about besides history homework."

Sphinx tilted back his chair and crossed his arms behind his head. "I knew it," he said. "Tropical islands, trips around the world, private planes. This is going to be the start of something great, you'll see!"

□

Sphinx was right about one thing: Treasure hunting fever was sweeping Philadelphia. By the next morning the school was buzzing with news about *Dragonstone*, the bookstores were selling out of copies and frantically ordering more, and the book was being passed from hand to hand, or—in some cases— jealously guarded. The newspapers were rushing to get interviews with the author. Sphinx appeared in the lunchroom brandishing copies of the *Guardian* and a few other papers. "Listen to this!" he crowed.

"Dr. Joyce Henning, author of the best seller *Dragonstone,* lives with her husband in a quiet house in Philadelphia's fashionable Main Line suburb," he read. "Recently retired as a professor of medieval history at the University of Pennsylvania, she has 'always wanted to write a book.' It took her just over three months to think up the clues that lead to the treasure, a valuable ring in the shape of a dragon studded with precious gems, which she has buried somewhere in or near the city. . . ."

"Joyce Henning is a wonder!" gushed a society columnist in another paper. "An absolute wonder! The celebrated author whose first book, *Dragonstone,* is causing ripples of excitement throughout Philadelphia first got the idea for her book while playing a game with her grandchildren. . . ."

"Dr. Joyce Henning, thin and elegant, lights a cigarette and settles back in her chair," reported the *Dispatch.* " 'I've always been fascinated by buried treasure,' she remarks. The smoke spirals up, lit by the long French windows behind her. A servant brings in a tea tray and arranges it on the table as we talk.

Q.: Dr. Henning, why exactly did you decide to write this book?

DR. HENNING: Well, one day I was looking at an antique brooch my mother had left me, and I thought what a good idea it would be to bury it somewhere and leave clues for the children to find it. [Dr. Henning has three grandchildren, ages twelve to eighteen.] I thought how much I would have enjoyed that at their age. And I did bury it, but they found it quite easily—the clues were too simple, you see—so I had to make it a bit harder. It was a game we played whenever they came to visit. They live in California, so they can't play the game from the book. I'm sure they'd be far too good at it anyway.

Q.: So you decided to write a book based on that experience.

DR. HENNING: Oh, yes, I thought it would be a lot of fun to put together some of the ideas I had come up with and publish a book of clues. I also used a much more valuable prize than I had in the game with the children—the dragon ring.

Q.: Did you expect your book to be a best seller?

DR. HENNING: Oh, no. My husband and I never expected the game to be so popular. Some of my former colleagues are shocked that this is how I am spending my retirement.

Q.: Would you describe this collection of clues as difficult or easy?

DR. HENNING: Well, rather difficult, I think. I didn't want to take all the adventure out of it by making the clues too easy, you know. They vary. However, as I mentioned in the book, the important thing is to look at them in the right way. That's the thing about clues, isn't it? Quite simple if you only know how to look at them. . . ."

"Sounds like a real character," Diggy said. "Okay. I went out last night and picked up copies of the book for all of us. They were going fast, I'm telling you." He distributed them around the lunch table. "Everybody owes me four dollars. Now, I think Sphinx is right. We'll divide the clues according to our best areas and take it from there. Who's good at what?"

Sphinx flipped through the pages. "There are eight clues, but the first is kind of a throwaway. The answer is obviously City Hall. She put it in the introduction, just to get everyone started."

"Okay, so that leaves seven—one for each of us, plus the last one, which we can all tackle together," said Diggy.

"I'll take any clue that has to do with history," Bobbie said.

Diggy thumbed through the book. "Number five."

"Fine."

"I'll take number seven, the mathematical one," Sphinx offered. "But I can't promise miracles. If I get into trouble, I'm going to have to call Frankie."

"I want number three," Chessie said firmly. "I don't have the slightest idea what it's about, but I love codes."

"I'll take my lucky number, six," Larry said.

"All right. That leaves two and four. Tilo?" said Diggy.

Tilo shook his head. "I don't know. Neither of them makes any sense to me. I sort of like the way number two looks, though. I'll take that one."

"Okay, so I'm number four. The clues build on

each other, so we'll need to get all of them. Everybody set?"

They nodded solemnly.

"Then go to it, and good luck!"

2

☐ That night Tilo sat hunched over his desk at home, his copy of *Dragonstone* open in front of him. He was reading the introduction for the third time.

> . . . each clue refers to a specific location in Philadelphia. Only by solving *all* the clues, however, can the dragon ring be found. All you need is a street map of Philadelphia. As you draw closer to the treasure you may want to see the places described by this book. They are all easy to reach.
>
> The first clue I will give you is simply to get you oriented in your search:
>
> > *Start at the center;*
> > *The center of the city,*
> > *The center of the government,*
> > *Will point you where you want to go.*

The following clues are more difficult, but everyone needs a starting point. . . .

Well, that is *simple enough,* Tilo thought. *It's City Hall, as Sphinx said.* He opened his street map and spread it out next to the book. City Hall was in the center of the map, the center of the city. *And it's the center of government all right,* Tilo thought. *Okay, that's where we start.* He circled the spot at Broad and Market streets and turned the page in his book.

Clue Number Two:

From the center
Go to the old center,
Then to the center of the old center and the
meetinghouse,

*Then to the center of the center and the center of the old
    center and the meetinghouse.*
Go slowly—don't be fooled!

Tilo exhaled. It looked the same way it had the day
before: like pure gibberish. He read it again, carefully.

From the center
Go to the old center . . .

Well, the center was probably City Hall, as in Clue
Number One. But the old center? He reached for the
map.

□

Chessie read Clue Number Three over again. She
too was seated at her desk, her glossy dark hair swinging just above the desk top as she leaned forward, her
elbows propped against the book. *Me and my big
mouth,* she thought. *'I love codes,' huh? Well, I'm usually
good at them, but this—just doesn't make any sense at all.
And with all that French homework to do. . . .*

Clue Number Three:

CGCBCDCBCDGABCG
NOTE THESE LETTERS WELL!

Note these letters well, Chessie thought. *Well, I'm doing
that, all right. Spending a lot more time on this treasure
hunt than I am on my schoolwork.* She glanced guiltily at
the pile of notebooks she had tossed on the floor to
make room for the book and map. Okay. Each clue
referred to a certain place in Philadelphia, so—the

name of the place might be spelled out by these letters if she could only find the key. It had to be some sort of alphabet code. Maybe if she switched the letters around. . . .

□

Diggy thrummed absently against the wall with his sneakers. His feet were up on his desk, and his chair was tilted dangerously backward. He yawned, stretched, and ran his hands through his tousled blond hair.

"Clue Number Four," he said out loud. "You cannot see the forest for the trees,/ Eleven of them all in a row." He sighed deeply and shrugged. "Eleven of them all in a row?" He tilted over backward until, his head arched upside down, he could just see the map of Philadelphia which he had drawn and pinned to the wall behind him. "Uh-huh." He dropped his feet to the floor and lowered his head down onto the desk. "I dunno," he mumbled.

□

Bobbie sat crouched in a big overstuffed armchair, her hands gripping the sides, the book in her lap. She stared at it as if it were an enemy.

Clue Number Five:

If our fifth President
Had stood in Thomas Jefferson's shoes,
Where would he be now?

Where would he be now? she thought, twirling one pigtail around her finger. Where would he be now?

She had already looked up the fifth President: it was James Monroe, 1758–1831. He had been President from 1817–1825. She had absently calculated how old he was when he died and how old he was when he was elected President. It was a habit of hers, when she was nervous, to collect these bits of information.

She was good at history, but she could never keep the Presidents straight. *Now, let's see, which President was Thomas Jefferson? Washington was the first, then, let's see . . .* she faltered. How embarrassing. Adams? Or was Jefferson next? Weren't there two Adamses? And what did all this have to do with a place in Philadelphia? It probably involved Independence Hall, where the Declaration of Independence was signed. But Monroe was only eighteen years old when the Declaration was signed. Was he there? She began to calculate nervously. How long was it between the signing of the Declaration of Independence and Monroe's becoming President?

□

Larry was stretched out on his bed, his chin on his fist, looking solemnly at the open book. At the top of the page was Clue Number Six.

All the roads to heaven are not on one map. Even rich uncles such as I seek other ways. Travel every path you will.

Not on one map . . . he mused. Maybe Joyce Henning meant that the treasure was hidden someplace that wouldn't be on a regular map of the city? No, that couldn't be right—that would be breaking the rules. Hmmm. Either there was a meaning hidden in the words themselves, or the clue was some kind of alphabet code. He picked up a pad and began to rearrange the letters of the message. He worked rapidly and neatly, but after an hour he gave up. It still made no sense.

□

Sphinx lay sprawled on his back on the bedroom floor. This was his favorite position for thinking.

He was convinced that he had gotten the toughest clue of all. This was what he wanted. *The bigger the challenge, the greater the glory when I win,* he thought. It never occurred to him that he might fail. After all this was a code, a difficult one, but still just a code. Math was Sphinx's specialty, his strongest subject.

He held up the notebook and looked again at the three rows of numbers that were Clue Number Seven:

> 17163034546267
> 12025395968828799
> 12040556974

That was it, just three lines of numbers. He had already tried to match them with the letters in the alphabet, *1* for *A* and so on down to *26* for *Z.* He had inserted spaces for the zeroes. This is what he had come up with:

> AGAFC CDEDFBFG
> AB BECIEIFHHBHGII
> AB D EEFIGD

That didn't help him any. Next he had tried taking the differences between every two neighboring numbers and seeing if they formed a meaningful sequence:

6653331112441
1223264432066120
1244501323

Oh, geez, he thought. *Doesn't look like anything.* He chewed on his ballpoint pen, doodled absently on his pad, managed to smear some ink on his left hand, and then substituted letters of the alphabet for the differences he had just calculated:

FFECCCAAABDDA
ABBCBFDDCB FFAB
ABDDE ACBC

He stared glumly at the result. Okay, so this retired professor, Joyce Whatever-her-name-was, was clever. There were no obvious leads. He hadn't really counted on that. He lay on the floor, eyes closed, his brain working furiously.

□

The next day in school Tilo came up to Diggy at his locker.

"Listen, Diggy. I've been thinking about this first clue, the one in the introduction. It's City Hall all right, but listen to this." He opened the book. " 'The center of the city,/ The center of the government,/ Will point you where you want to go.' You know that statue of William Penn on top of City Hall? Well, he's pointing somewhere. I don't know where, but I think that's what Dr. Henning might have meant."

Diggy leaned against his locker and brushed his hair out of his eyes. "Mmm-huh. You may be right." He glanced down at his watch. "I have to get to class now, but maybe you and I could go after school and take a look?"

"I'll meet you on the steps."

A few hours later they were walking uptown toward Broad and Market. At first they chattered about school that day, but then there was a long silence. Tilo finally glanced sideways with a grin. "Any luck with your clue?" he asked.

Diggy shook his head. "Nope. I spent most of last night on it instead of my homework. I can see that this treasure hunt is going to be an even bigger distraction than I thought."

"Yes," Tilo said. "I worked on mine until my head was spinning."

"Did you get anywhere?"

"Nowhere at all."

"Well," Diggy said, "it'll take time. I think Sphinx is stumped too. Serves him right, after all the noise he made about it. Look, there's City Hall."

The many-storied gray stone structure rose above its square court at Broad and Market streets. At the very top stood a statue of William Penn, his right hand out, fingers spread as if in blessing. The boys circled the building.

"Let's see, his right hand points pretty much

northeast," Tilo said. He turned to look out over that section of town. "What is he pointing to? Independence Hall isn't in that direction."

"Yet another choice bit of city history we don't know. Maybe he's pointing toward New York?"

"He's not even really pointing, now that I see it close up," Tilo said. "Maybe I'm wrong, but he seems to be speaking and making a gesture."

"Well, it can't hurt to know that he *might* be pointing toward the treasure, or toward one of the clues at least. Okay, let's go home."

□

The phone rang. Sphinx picked it up. "Leave me alone," he snarled. "I'm working."

"Touchy. Very touchy," said a girl's amused voice. "It's Chessie, Sphinx. I recognize you by your lovely telephone manners. Listen, Diggy and Tilo want me to relay something to you. They went to look at the statue of Billy Penn on top of City Hall today. They think it might have something to do with the first clue. Do you have your map handy?"

"What do you think?" Sphinx said with a groan.

"Well, the statue points northeast. Got it? Northeast. They wanted us all to know in case it helped with the other clues."

"Great," said Sphinx, scanning the map rapidly. "What's it pointing to—the bus station? That leaves the entire northeastern section of Philadelphia and its suburbs open. Wow. That really narrows it down."

"Well, that's *our* job, isn't it? Speaking of which, how are things going for you?"

"Couldn't be worse. I'm in a complete fog."

"Yeah, well"—Chessie's voice softened—"me too. But maybe Tilo is on to something. See you tomorrow."

☐

From the center
Go to the old center,
Then to the center of the old center and the
  meetinghouse,
Then to the center of the center and the center of the old
  center and the meetinghouse.

Tilo groaned. His back ached from bending over the map.

The center was City Hall. Okay, so the old center must be . . . What had been the center of government before the present one? His finger hovered over Independence Hall at Fifth and Chestnut. Suddenly he gave a low whistle. Right next to Independence Hall was a tiny square labeled Old City Hall! Why hadn't he seen that before? So *that* was the old center.

Okay, he thought, *now I'm getting somewhere.*

☐

Chessie had tried substituting numbers for all the letters according to their position in the alphabet. She had read the code backward and forward and had counted up how many times each letter appeared. She had taken the differences between all the neighboring numbers and turned them back into letters again. Nothing made any sense at all. She was at a dead end. Discouraged, she slumped over her desk. Why had she let Sphinx talk her into this stupid treasure hunt anyway? She had better things to do than figure out some kind of moronic code. She swept the book and map off her desk, took out her homework, and settled down to work.

Half an hour later she was going over the map inch by inch, checking out the northeastern part of the city. . . .

□

Bobbie found herself calculating Thomas Jefferson's life-span (eighty-three years) and age at which he was elected President (fifty-seven years). She leaned back with a sigh. This wasn't helping at all.

□

The next day in school Sphinx wore a deep scowl. Diggy glanced at him during class.

"What's the problem, Sphinx? You look awful."

"Thanks."

"The clue, huh?"

"Yeah. Do you know what I did most of last night? I subtracted all the numbers from each other until they all disappeared. Then I divided them into each other. Then I multiplied them all together. Then I practically took the *square roots* to see if that would help. The result? Nothing. Absolutely nothing."

"We've only been working on this for two days," Diggy said. "Give yourself some time. Nobody else has had any luck, you know."

Sphinx's scowl deepened. "I intend to be the first. I thought it up, didn't I? I can tell, everybody else will solve their clues, and I'll be the only one who can't. Think of the humiliation."

Diggy regarded him quizzically. "It's not a competition, Sphinx. Anyway, you always have Frankie to help you."

"Yeah, well, in a few days I'll be knocking on Chessie's door, asking her little brother to come out and solve a few equations for me."

□

Bobbie and Chessie walked home from school together that day. Chessie was restless, kicking at pebbles on the cobblestone streets, her pretty face set in a frown.

"I don't like what's happening to us," she said. "It's only been a few days since we started this silly treasure hunt, and already the gang is drawing apart. You know, all of us spending all our time on our own clues. I don't like it."

Bobbie tucked a strand of blond hair behind her ear. She had recently started wearing her hair down, out of her old braids, and it was always getting in her eyes. "Oh, you're too worried about it. So everyone's competitive. That's okay. It'd be strange if it were any other way. Or," she added teasingly, "are you worried that one *particular* boy isn't paying enough attention to you?"

Chessie flushed. "No, it's not Diggy," she answered honestly. "It's Sphinx mainly. And the others. I don't have a good feeling about it. Maybe we ought to call the whole thing off?"

"I think it's a little late for that," Bobbie said. "The boys are too into it, and to tell you the truth, so am I."

Chessie shrugged. "Maybe it's just that I feel so frustrated with my own clue. I've tried everything I can think of."

Bobbie made an exasperated sound as her hair blew into her face, and raising her arms, she began to braid it down the back. "Had enough of this for one day," she muttered. "Listen, don't let it get to you, Chess. Remember what the author said, that it's easy when you look at it the right way. It'll hit you, I know it will."

"I guess so. Want to come over to my house for a while?"

"Oh, I'd love to, Chess, but I have to go work on my clue."

Chessie swung around. "You see? This is just the sort of thing—" she began furiously.

"I'm *teasing* you," Bobbie said, linking arms with her. "Boy, are you touchy. Come on, let's go to your place. Frankie hasn't had a chance to annoy me for days."

□

"Whoever you are, I don't want to talk to you," Sphinx said into the phone that evening.

"Charming," Bobbie said. "Absolutely charming. I'm beginning to think that Chessie is right. This treasure hunt is making everybody crazy. I called up to see if you wanted to trade clues for a while and brainstorm. Interested?"

"I don't know a thing about history, Bobbie."

"So you'll be of no use to me at all. That's okay. Chessie's worried that the gang is drawing apart because of these clues, and I wanted to make her feel better. Anyway, I feel as if I haven't really talked to any of you guys recently."

Sphinx chewed on his pen. "Okay. It's not such a bad idea. I could use a break from these numbers. I'll think about history for a while. Why don't you come over now?"

"On my way."

Half an hour later she was perched on the end of Sphinx's bed while Sphinx sprawled on the floor, the map open in front of him. Bobbie was scribbling on a pad of paper.

"What are you so busy at?" Sphinx asked irritably.

"Oh, I like to subtract. I do it when I get nervous."

"Don't bother. I've already subtracted everything from everything. I've also added everything to everything, divided everything into everything, and done just about anything I could think of to those numbers except wring their tiny little necks." He turned back to Clue Number Five. "If our fifth President/Had stood in Thomas Jefferson's shoes,/Where would he be now?" he intoned. "Ummmm . . . Monticello? That was Jefferson's home."

"Be quiet, Sphinx. I'm trying to work."

"I don't even know who our fifth President was."

"James Monroe. Do you know he lived to be seventy-three years old?"

"Really? That's great." He looked down at the book. "Does that have anything to do with this?"

"No."

"Oh." He scratched his arm reflectively. "And Thomas Jefferson was our, umm, *third* President, right?"

"That's right." Bobbie put down her pad. "That's pretty impressive, Sphinx."

He waved his hand airily. "It's nothing. I've been in school for nearly ten years now. So if our fifth President had stood in our third President's shoes . . . Geez, I don't know."

"Well, don't let anyone say you didn't try." Bobbie turned back to her work. "Now leave me alone. I want to see what I can do here."

"I thought this was supposed to be the social hour," Sphinx complained, but he went back to the book.

Two hours later, thoroughly discouraged, they gave up. "Thanks anyway, Sphinx," Bobbie said. "It helped get my mind off my own clue for a little while."

"It's okay, Bobbie. Drop by anytime. You know where to find me. I'll be sitting right here looking at this book. When I start clawing the walls and they take me away, will you come visit me?"

"Yeah, you can count on it."

□

Tilo was conscious of a mounting sense of excitement. The old center was Old City Hall, so there had to be a meetinghouse somewhere nearby. His finger traced a wavering line around the Independence Mall area, which extended for several blocks around Old City Hall.

He exhaled softly. There!

The Free Quaker Meeting House was just a few blocks away to the north. So the center of the old center and the meetinghouse would have to be . . . And the center of the center and the center of the old center and the meetinghouse was . . .

As the clue cautioned, he went slowly through the confusing words and was rewarded by a sudden wave of relief. His thin face lit up with a smile of triumph. *He had it!*

3

☐ Tilo raced into school the next day. He sat impatiently through homeroom and then cornered Diggy in his first class.

"I've got it," he said. "I figured out the clue!"

"You're kidding! That's great! What's the answer?"

"Tell you later," Tilo whispered as the teacher turned to look at them. "At lunch."

The gang met in the cafeteria and cleared off a table. Tilo spread out a map.

" 'From the center/Go to the old center,' " he said. "The center is City Hall—we figured that out from the first clue—so the old center must be Old City Hall, next to Independence Hall." He tapped it with his finger. "Now *here*"—his finger moved north—"is the Free Quaker Meeting House, at Fifth and Arch streets. So I figure the center of the old center and the meetinghouse must be *halfway* between Old City Hall

and the Free Quaker Meeting House, here"—his finger moved down—"at Fifth and Market. That would
put it on a dead line with City Hall at Broad and
Market, nine blocks away." His finger moved down
Market Street to stop at City Hall. "Okay. So that
means—here it gets really confusing, but just listen as
I go through it slowly—that means that the center is
City Hall, and the center of the old center and the
meetinghouse is Fifth and Market. So in line four of
the clue you take the center of those two places,
which is *here*"—his finger jabbed at the map—"between Ninth and Tenth on Market. Do you get it?"

"No," said Larry.

"Okay, look." Tilo pulled a pad of paper toward
him and sat down, the gang gathering around him.
"It's clear once you see it. Here's City Hall, the
center in line one." He drew it on the page. "You
have to remember that the centers keep shifting.
Now here's Old City Hall, the center in line two."
He drew a square a few inches away and down.

"Now here's the meetinghouse."

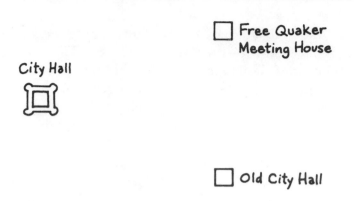

"So the center of the old center and the meetinghouse is halfway between them, here."

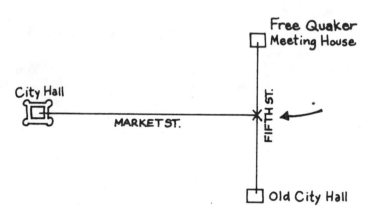

"And the spot halfway between City Hall and the center of the old center and the meetinghouse is *here*, around Tenth and Market. That's the new center referred to in line four. Do you see?"

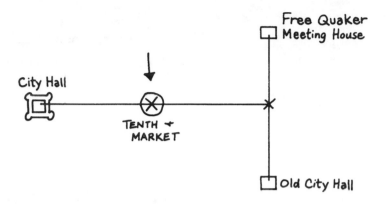

He passed the paper around, and the other kids examined it, nodding.

"Good work, Tilo," Larry said. "That's a hard one, all right."

"I see it now," said Bobbie.

Sphinx remained silent.

"What's at Tenth and Market?" Diggy asked.

"I don't know," Tilo replied. "I'm going after school today to find out."

Diggy took out his map. He put a circle around City Hall and another halfway between Ninth and Tenth on Market Street. "We have two clues answered now," he said. "Can I go with you this afternoon, Tilo? I'm curious to see what's there."

"Me too," said Chessie.

"I can't go," Larry said. "I'm working on props for the play. There's a meeting after school. There *are* some things on my mind besides this treasure hunt, you know."

"I can't go either," Sphinx said. "I'm busy." He drained his cup and stood up. "Call me at home tonight if you find anything interesting." He walked away.

Chessie's eyes followed him thoughtfully.

"I can't go either," Bobbie said, breaking the silence. "Well, I *can't,*" she said, catching Chessie's glance. "I have lacrosse practice today."

"Okay, so it's the three of us," Diggy said, folding up the map. "Let's meet on the steps after school."

□

Tilo stood on the corner of Ninth and Market and glanced up and down the street. "All right," he said. "There's the post office, and beyond that a row of stores."

"Okay," said Diggy, scribbling in his notebook.

"And on the other side is a big department store," Chessie said. "It takes up the whole block."

"Maybe this is what she meant," Tilo said, gazing at the post office building, "but the spot on the map is really farther down." They walked toward Tenth Street. "Just stores on either side. Could the clue be referring to these?"

"No idea," Diggy said. "Maybe Joyce Henning has a favorite store somewhere around here. Who knows. Well, at least we've got some idea of what's on this block now."

"Maybe I've got the whole thing wrong," Tilo said. "Maybe the clue wasn't referring to this at all."

"Don't be silly. Your answer makes sense," Chessie

said sharply. "I'm sure you're right." But her eyes lingered on the line of stores as they turned to leave.

"It could be the post office," Diggy guessed. "That's a definite landmark. We'll have to wait and see. Assuming, of course, that the rest of us can come up with answers as quickly as you did, Tilo!"

□

That night Sphinx concentrated fiercely on his clue. He went over the map carefully and scribbled jumbled lines of numbers across a memo pad.

When the pad was full and he was too tired to think clearly, he lay down on his bed. He still held a piece of paper covered with scrawled notations. He gazed at it for a moment. Then with a sound of disgust he tore it up and scattered it all over the room.

□

The next day was Saturday. Usually on weekends the gang would meet at someone's house and have dinner together or go to a movie. But today nobody suggested getting together. That evening Mrs. Strauss came to the door of Larry's room and regarded her son as he worked at his desk.

"Such application," she said wryly. "Such diligence. I've never seen anything like it. A new project?"

"Sort of."

"Uh-huh. Well, I wanted to tell you that if you'd like to invite the gang over tonight or tomorrow, that's all right with us."

"Thanks, but, ummm, I don't think so. Not this

weekend. Y'see, I'm kind of busy, and we're all working on projects—*separate* projects. I don't think it'd be a good idea."

Mrs. Strauss lifted her eyebrows. "Separate projects, is that it?" She walked over to her son's desk and took the copy of *Dragonstone* out of his hands. She regarded it coolly. "I see."

□

On Sunday afternoon Chessie phoned Diggy. "I've had it," she said. "I'm tired of being alone. Are you working on your clue?"

"What else?"

"Would you like to come over and work on it here?"

"Sure, Chess. I'll be by in a little while."

When he arrived, she had already cleared off the table. Frankie was hanging over the back of a chair.

"Chessie hasn't been able to get her clue," he announced smugly as Diggy came in. "She hasn't even got close."

"Oh, yeah? Well, neither have I, squirt," Diggy said. "So you'd better stay out of my way."

"Chessie doesn't have a chance of getting it," the eight-year-old said. "She told me it doesn't make any sense at all."

His sister shooed him away. "Oh, for goodness' sake, Frankie," she said as he backed into a coffee table. "Please leave before you break everything in the room." She settled into a chair and pulled her note pad toward her. "I wish we had never started this," she said to Diggy. "I really do. I'm seeing these letters in my sleep."

"Well, one thing's for sure, I figure I'll never get lost in Philadelphia again," he replied. "I've been over this map so many times I could find my way around now blindfolded."

"The only one who's having a decent weekend is Tilo."

"Not really. Nobody else is talking to him."

"You don't mean the others are shutting him out?" Chessie said.

"Oh, no, nothing that obvious. But Sphinx is eating his heart out that he wasn't the one to get it first. And Larry's not much better."

Chessie shook her head. "I don't know. I'm having trouble getting into this whole thing."

"Really? I'm having trouble getting *out* of it. I think about my clue all day long."

An hour later they took a break. Diggy picked up the pad Chessie had been working on.

"Why don't we switch for a while?" he suggested. "Give our brains something new to think about."

"I'm game." She took Diggy's scratch paper. It was covered with words that looked as if they had been written at random, loose doodlings, a drawing of a tree, a rough sketch of some kind of monkey, and a small, perfect map of Philadelphia.

"Sorry," Diggy said, glancing over her shoulder. "When I get bored, I draw whatever I'm looking at. The teacher, my lab apparatus, or in this case, Philadelphia."

"Yes? When did you see this?" Chessie pointed to the monkey.

"Oh, that's just a doodle. Don't let it worry you." He sat back. "You know, I have a feeling that both these clues are the kind that you either get in one step, or not at all. Not like Tilo's, where you can work it out bit by bit. It must be that we're just not looking at it right."

"Surprise," Chessie said bitterly. "I already had a feeling I wasn't looking at it right."

There was silence for a while as they struggled with the new clues. Chessie pulled the map toward her. Then she looked up, guiltily.

"I don't know how to tell you this, but I think I've solved your clue."

Diggy stared at her. "Oh, great! And how long did it take—half an hour? After I've been looking at it for days?"

"Well, look," she said, hitching her chair over toward his. " 'You cannot see the forest for the trees,/ Eleven of them all in a row.' The key word is *forest*. I was looking at the map, and it made me think of the Forrest Theatre. At Eleventh and Walnut." She pointed.

"You're right," Diggy said. "You're right. Eleven walnut trees. It's . . . so simple!"

Chessie's lips twitched. "Only if you look at it the right way, as I remember someone saying earlier."

"The Forrest Theatre." Diggy circled the spot on the map. "Okay, Chessie. I'm sitting here until I get your clue."

Chessie laughed. "Okay."

Diggy looked around as Frankie ran into the room. "Hey, listen, Frankie. Your sister just solved my clue. What do you think of that?"

Frankie put his hands on his hips and regarded Diggy gravely. "Wow. You must be *really* dumb." He was out of the room before his sister could say anything.

They sat at the table for another hour, Diggy working hard, Chessie absorbed in a novel. Finally Diggy leaned back with a sigh. "Well, I'm not sure now," he said, handing her a piece of paper, "but I think you've been going at it wrong, trying to fit these letters into some kind of alphabet code. I don't think they're letters at all—not in the usual sense."

"What are they?"

"I think they're notes." He jabbed a finger at *Dragonstone.* " '*Note* these letters well.' I figure they must be musical notes, not words at all."

"Notes?" Chessie said in exasperation. "After all that time I spent . . ." She rapidly scanned the paper in her hand. "Well, there's one way to find out."

She walked into the living room and over to the old, broken-down piano that her mother had lovingly saved from her own childhood.

"Can you play?" asked Diggy.

"No, not really, but enough to pick this out." She sat down briskly and glanced at the book. "C—G—C —B—C."

The front door opened, and they could hear her parents coming in.

Chessie grimly picked out the notes. "Ummm, let's see. D—C—B—C—D—G—A—B—C—G. Does that sound like anything to you, Diggy?"

"Not to me, no. But, then, I'm no music genius."

"Neither'm I. Well, it could be something. Let's try again." She began over again.

She was halfway through when suddenly, from the next room, they heard a deep male voice pick up the melody.

"La la la laaa . . ." roared Mr. Morelli, appearing dramatically at the entrance to the living room. "La la la laaaaa laaaaa. . . ." He stopped when he saw their astonished faces.

"Schubert's Unfinished Symphony," he said. "Right, honey? One of my all-time favorites. Never knew you knew it." He turned and headed toward the kitchen, still bellowing. "La laaaa la la la laaaaaa . . ."

4

□ "It's a lopsided square," Bobbie said, looking over Diggy's shoulder. The gang had met in school the next day, and Diggy was showing them the clues he and Chessie had solved.

"Yeah," he said, frowning. "Doesn't look like much, does it? City Hall, that spot at Tenth and Market, and now the Forrest and Shubert theaters."

"You must have been thrilled when your father knew that song," Tilo said to Chessie.

"We couldn't believe it," she replied. "He just appeared at the door, sang the rest of the theme, and then turned and left. We stood there like two idiots. It didn't hit us until later that it meant the Shubert Theatre. We had to go back to the map and look around a bit."

"Pretty impressive," Sphinx said. "I'd never have known they were musical notes."

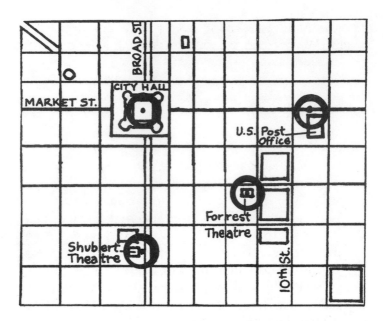

"Me neither," Chessie said. "I'd have been banging my head against the wall forever." She stopped suddenly, looking at Sphinx with a troubled expression on her face.

"Yeah, well," mumbled Sphinx, turning away, "I know what that's like."

"So we have a strange-looking square, or a really weird-looking circle," Diggy was saying. "Where does that get us?"

"Anything interesting inside these four points?" Larry asked.

"Nothing that leaps up and screams, 'I'm the place where she hid the treasure!'" Diggy said dryly.

"Chessie and I looked it over pretty thoroughly last night. We decided we should go take a look around there. Everybody up for that?"

"Sure," said Bobbie, and the others agreed. "After school today," she said. "We'll walk around and see what we can find."

"It doesn't make sense to go there if we don't know what we're looking for," Tilo objected.

"Well, it looks like our search is narrowing down to somewhere in here," Diggy said, indicating the four points on the map. "It can't hurt to take a look."

They met on the steps after school and walked uptown. First they went to City Hall and walked around it once. "I don't care if he *is* pointing northeast," Sphinx confided to Chessie. "I still don't think it has anything to do with the treasure." Then they headed down Broad Street toward the Shubert Theatre. They had decided they would look at the four points first. From the Shubert they walked to the Forrest Theatre, and from there up Eleventh Street, then over to Tenth and Market. They stopped on the corner indicated by Tilo's clue and chatted for a while. Tilo was looking around doubtfully.

"I just hope I was right," he said.

"Let's walk back that way," Diggy said. He pointed southwest, toward Twelfth and Walnut, roughly at the center of the lopsided square formed by the four points.

"Okay." Chessie was holding her map and copy of *Dragonstone*. She looked up to see a stranger nearby watching her. "Look, Diggy, there's somebody else with a copy of the book!" She waved, and the man courteously lifted his hat before walking away. He turned around once to look back at the teenagers, then disappeared around the corner.

"He must've figured out my clue," Tilo said uneasily.

"Have you seen anyone else with the book?" Chessie asked.

They shook their heads. "It's not surprising somebody else is here," Diggy said. "We're bound to meet more and more treasure hunters as we get closer."

"Assuming, of course, that we do get closer," Sphinx said gloomily.

Bobbie took his arm. "Look, Sphinx, here's your favorite sort of place—a playground!"

Sphinx brightened. "With *swings!*"

She steered him away from the group. Diggy gave a low whistle. "That's something new, isn't it?"

Chessie shook her head, her long dark hair swinging. "I think she's worried about him. He's so gloomy these days."

They walked around that section of the town for a while. It was like any other downtown part of a city —bustling, crowded with people and cars. There were no Gothic cathedrals, no ancient graveyards with leaning tombstones, no odd-looking villains bent on leading them off the trail. After an hour and a half Chessie sat down on a bench with a sigh.

"Enough," she said. "I've seen more of midtown than I ever wanted to see in my life. Let's go home."

Larry had his copy of *Dragonstone* out and was

thumbing through it when he was startled by a whistle nearby. The gang looked up to see four boys, a
few years older, on the other side of the street. One of
them was waving *Dragonstone.*

"We've seen you around!" he called. "You'd better
give up, we're going to get it first!"

Larry waved his copy in the air. "No way!" he
shouted. "We already know where it is! We're just
doing this to throw everyone else off the track!"

The boys looked at each other. One of them crossed
the street and came up to the gang. "I'm not kidding," he said. "My friends and I are going to get the
treasure first. I mean it." There was no doubt that he
did mean it.

Diggy stepped forward. "Are you threatening us?"

"No. I'm telling you not to waste your time. What
are you, in junior high school?" He laughed. "You
don't have a chance. Just give up and let the adults do
it. This is no game for little kids. Go play with something else—okay?"

"Well, now, Frankie would be really offended,"
Sphinx remarked. "If we're little kids, he must be
completely out of the running."

"Listen, we'll do whatever we want," Diggy told
the older boy. "We don't need anyone's approval, es-
pecially not yours."

The other boy regarded him thoughtfully. "Okay,"
he said. "I don't want to get into a fight about it. I just
thought I'd save you some trouble. It's not worth ar-
guing about." He loped across the street to rejoin his
friends.

"What a moron!" Chessie said.

"Never mind," said Diggy. "We're ready to go home anyway."

"I think that settles it," Sphinx said, looking first at Bobbie and then at Larry. "We three are going to get our clues, *fast*—before those guys over there—or we're going to kill ourselves trying. Right?"

□

It couldn't be a code based on frequency of occurrence of the letters, Larry decided that night for the tenth time. The clue was too short to contain any meaningful frequencies. And the words themselves didn't seem to have much meaning. It had to be an alphabet code of some kind, and it just couldn't be anything really elaborate. The clue was too short for that.

Fine, he thought. *Now I can go ahead and feel* really *stupid.*

An alphabet code had been one of his first ideas, and he had pages of letter combinations to prove it. But nothing had made any sense.

He picked up one of the pages, his first. He had shifted the letters in the code forward one position in the alphabet, then backward one. Then forward two and backward two. Then forward three and so on. He had stopped when he found himself trying to shift all the letters forward eleven, which put several letters past the end of the alphabet. He sighed and crumpled up the paper in his fist.

□

"Surprise!" Bobbie said.

She had showed up at Sphinx's front door with a tinfoil-wrapped package in her hand.

"I like it, whatever it is," Sphinx said. He let her in, and she set the plate on the kitchen table. "It's a cake," she said. "Chocolate cream with strawberry jam filling. One of your favorites, right?"

"Anything that goes by the name of cake is my favorite," Sphinx said. "It looks great, Bobbie. Want some? Or is it all for me?"

"My goodness, you're a pig."

"What is it, my birthday or something? A national holiday? Have I won a prize?"

"None of the above." Bobbie took two plates from the cupboard and cut a piece for each of them. She handed his to him and said carefully, "I came over to tell you that everyone thinks you're acting like a total jerk."

Sphinx frowned. "I see. The cake's to sweeten the message?"

"Uh-hmmm." She seated herself and regarded him seriously. "Look, Sphinx. We've been friends for a long time. What's going on with you?"

"Nothing."

"I see. Then why are you acting like not getting your clue is the end of the world?"

Sphinx scowled at his cake. "I'm not."

"I think you are."

"I'm not!" He stood up and irritably began to pace the room. "Look, Bobbie, it's important to me. That's all. I thought up the whole idea. I got everyone interested in it. Now everybody's going to get their clue before I do. It bothers me, that's all. There's nothing fancy about it. Satisfied?"

There was a silence.

"Not really," Bobbie said. "You're making everybody feel guilty about solving their clues. It's stupid, Sphinx. We have to solve *all* the clues. So what if you're not the first? That doesn't mean you'll be the last."

"I will," Sphinx moaned. "I can tell."

Bobbie looked at him in disgust, then handed him a fork. "Here, take this. Somehow I think you'll survive."

He shook his head. "All right, all right, you win. I'll behave from now on. Tell the others you've reformed me."

"Eat now, reform later," Bobbie said.

□

Larry looked doubtfully at the sheet of paper on the desk. He had scrawled "lines and columns" at the top. Maybe if he could arrange the twenty-four words of the clue in a certain order, the solution could be read directly either in the first letters or the last letters of each line, or in a given vertical column. The hard part would be finding out what arrangement gave a clear message.

He started by putting one word per line. As soon as he saw:

All
The
Roads
To
Heaven

he knew he was on the wrong trail. *Atrth* wasn't exactly an English word; it sounded like something in Martian. And the other columns were all wrong too.

He sighed and began to rearrange the words once again.

□

Bobbie solved her clue the next day. She was in the middle of a science experiment when she stumbled and dropped a flask full of boiling red liquid. Sphinx, her lab partner, stared at her.

"What's the matter?" he asked. "It's *my* responsibility to mess up in here. And," he added, stooping to clean up, "I take my responsibilities seriously."

Bobbie managed to look exultant and guilty at the same time. "I have it. I just got the answer to the clue."

Sphinx got slowly to his feet, a pan of broken glass in his hand.

"The clues are the *third* President and the name *Monroe,*" Bobbie said, her eyes glazed. "The third President, Jefferson. If our fifth President, James Monroe, had stood in Jefferson's shoes, where would he be? *Third and Monroe!*"

"Monroe? I didn't even know there was a street with that name."

"Yeah, there is." Bobbie ran to her desk and fumbled for her map. "It's near where Tilo lives, around South Street. Oh, I'm sorry, Sphinx, let me do that," she said, grabbing some paper towels and kneeling down. "Careful of the glass. Oh, what a mess."

"I'll say," Sphinx replied, deep in gloom.

Bobbie gave him a long look. "Remember what you told me yesterday, Sphinx."

"I remember. See how cheerful I am? A whole new leaf." He was unfolding the map. "Let's see. Third and Monroe is—right here. And that means . . ." There was a pause, then a low whistle. "Bobbie, I don't believe it! Look at this!"

"What is it?" She scrambled to her feet just as the science teacher glanced in their direction.

"Bobbie. Oliver," he said, "I understand that a broken flask is a momentary crisis, but by all means don't let it stop your work for the whole afternoon."

"Sorry," Sphinx mumbled. Folding up the map, he whispered to Bobbie, *"Show you later."*

□

"We thought the clues formed a circle or a square on the map," Bobbie said. The gang had gathered at Diggy's house after school that day. Bobbie stood in front of the map pinned to his bedroom wall. "But that didn't narrow it down much, as our walk yesterday proved. We also thought the first clue, 'The center of the city/Will point you where you want to go,' meant that statue of Billy Penn. Sphinx thought all along that that was misleading, and he was right."

50

She turned to the map. "Look. When I add the fifth spot, at Third and Monroe, what do all the clues form?"

"A kite?" said Tilo.

"A cross?" said Chessie.

"No, look again!" Bobbie sketched rapidly, connecting the points. "It's an *arrow!* With City Hall as the point. 'The center of the city/Will *point* you where you want to go'—get it?"

"I don't know," Tilo said. "It still looks like a kite to me."

"Oh, Bobbie, good going," Chessie said. "That's it, all right."

They stared silently at the arrow. "It's pointing straight up the Benjamin Franklin Parkway," Larry said, chewing his lip. "Toward . . . ?"

"Toward nothing," Sphinx finished. "We don't know yet. It's up to you and me now, Larry. The last two clues."

"Right." Larry sighed. "And I'm exactly nowhere on it."

"And I'm right behind you."

□

"Larry," Mrs. Levanthal called out in class the next day, "will you please conjugate the verb *avoir* for us?"

"Oh, geez," Larry muttered under his breath, pulling his French textbook over a piece of paper on which he had written "All the roads to heaven." "Yes, okay. Ummm . . . *J'ai. Tu as. Il a. Nous avons. Vous avez. . . . Ils ont.*"

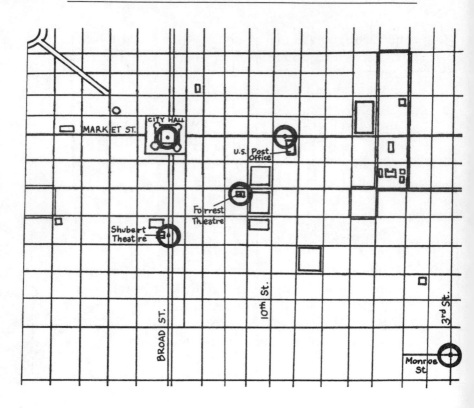

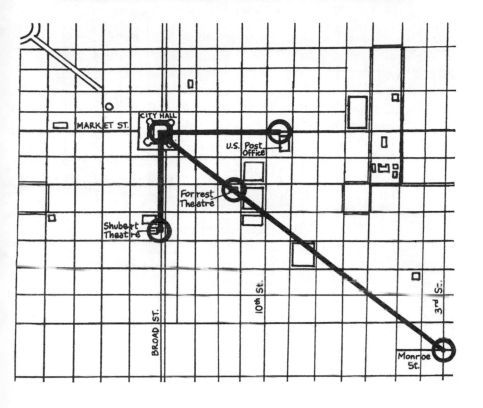

"Second person singular imperfect. First person plural conditional. Third person singular future," the teacher drilled, moving across the classroom toward him.

Larry hesitated, floundering, and Chessie, seated behind him, prodded him in the back. *"Il aura,"* she whispered.

"No help, please, Chessie," Mrs. Levanthal said. She stopped in front of Larry's desk. "Do you have your homework for today, Larry?"

"No, I'm afraid I don't."

Mrs. Levanthal looked at him thoughtfully. "Something else on your mind?"

"Not exactly. Well, I guess you could say that."

"All right. Get your homework in tomorrow, Larry. You've been unprepared for the last few classes. Don't think I don't notice. Now, class, *exercice numéro dix . . .*"

Larry slumped in his chair, doodling absentmindedly on his notebook cover. Chessie leaned forward and whispered, "You're lucky you got off that easy."

Larry pretended he had not heard. *What I need right now,* he thought, *is a rich uncle, like in the clue. Then I wouldn't have to be beating my head against a wall in this treasure hunt.*

That night he swept his French homework off the desk before settling down to work. *French irregular verbs will just have to wait,* he thought grimly. *I can't let Sphinx beat me on this one.*

Some of the scrap paper from the last two days' work was still on the desk. He picked it up, read it, and dropped it into the waste paper basket. *Useless,* he thought. *Well, at least it shows me a lot of blind alleys I don't have to go up again.*

He took a fresh piece of paper from the drawer and wrote:

All the
Roads to
Heaven are
Not on
One map.

Maybe this is another dead end, he thought miserably. He looked at the first column: *arhno.* And the second column: *loeon.* Something was definitely wrong. It sounded like Martian again. Maybe he was doing this all backward.

What I need is a computer, he thought. It could shuffle the words around until it hit something that made sense.

The idea of shuffling words around triggered an idea in Larry's mind. He ran downstairs to the basement and searched till he found what he was looking for: two old Scrabble sets. Back in his room he arranged the letters on one of the boards to form the clue message. Then he began to move the Scrabble pieces around, first single letters, then whole words, lining up the columns to see if they made any sense.

After an hour he began to smile.

5

□ "Once I got the Scrabble sets, it wasn't too bad," Larry told the others at lunch the next day. "Really, now that I see it, I could kick myself for not getting it earlier."

He showed them a pad of paper, on which he had written:

All the roads	tO
Heaven are not	oN
One map. Even	ricH
Uncles such as	I
Seek other ways.	TraveL
Every path you	wilL.

"Six lines, four words per line," Larry said proudly. "Read down the first and last columns."

"A house on hill," Chessie read in a puzzled tone.

"But what hill? What does this have to do with our other clues?"

"I wasn't sure at first," Larry said. "I was pretty annoyed, thinking it wasn't much help at all. It's so vague: 'A house on hill.' But look." He grabbed the map on which the five points had been connected by an arrow with its point at City Hall. "Look. You follow the arrow up the Benjamin Franklin Parkway"—his finger traced the line—"until you end up at a house on a hill." His finger came to rest at the upper lefthand corner of the map. "*Here.* Riverhill Mansion, right behind the art museum!"

"Oh, wow," mumbled Diggy. "I can't believe it. We're actually getting close."

Larry tapped the spot. "I'm positive that's where we'll find the ring!"

"That's it, all right," Sphinx said. "We've got to get out there quick."

"After school today," Diggy said. "Can everyone make it? Okay. Good work, Larry."

"It was nothing," Larry replied. "It took me nearly two weeks of solid work and will probably cost me my grades in every class I have."

□

When the bell rang and the lunch meeting broke up, Sphinx went to his next class sunk in deep gloom. Bobbie slid into a seat next to him and looked at him anxiously.

"How're you doing?" she asked.

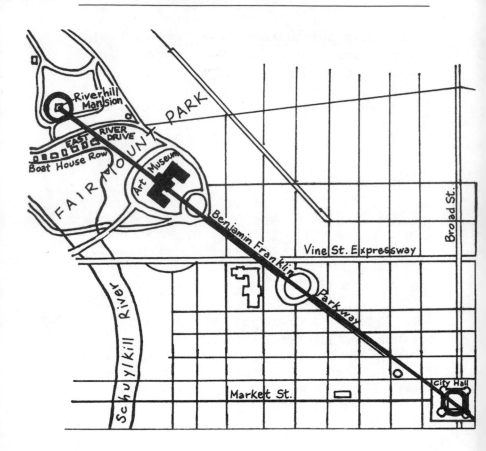

"You mean, how am I doing now that I'm officially the last one to get my clue?" Sphinx asked savagely.

Bobbie pursed her lips. "Yes, that's what I mean."

"Perhaps you mean," amended Sphinx, "how am I feeling now that absolutely everyone else has solved their clues except for me, *and* I haven't done any homework in two weeks, *and* I'll probably flunk out of school this semester?"

"Yes, I guess that's what I mean."

"You mean," he asked deliberately, "how am I feeling now that everyone else has solved their clues, and I haven't done any homework in two weeks, and I'll probably flunk out of school, *and* I don't have any self-respect left because here this thing was all my idea, and now I can't even solve the stupid *clue?!*"

"Why, yes, Sphinx, I think that's what I'm asking you," Bobbie said, drumming her fingers angrily on the desk top. "Just how do you feel now?"

"Fine," Sphinx snarled, "just fine." He slammed his notebook down on the desk as the teacher, with a startled look in his direction, called the class to order.

□

After their last class the gang went to the nearest bus stop and caught the bus uptown. "This'll take us up the parkway," Diggy said, settling into his seat. "Into Fairmount Park. We'll have to walk once we get there."

After a twenty-minute ride the bus let them off at the base of a small slope. They walked up the hill. At the top it leveled off into a broad, beautiful lawn which swept away from them in a curve, ending in a thicket of woods at the edge of a cliff. In front of them and slightly to the left was the mansion.

It was a Gothic structure, three stories high, with turrets, narrow windows, and long balconies. There was a modern brick addition tacked awkwardly on to one end.

"Wow," said Chessie. "All it needs is a moat."

"Let's check out those woods at the end," Diggy said.

They crossed the lawn, which ended abruptly in an outcropping of jagged stone. Behind the stone was a small woods, which continued right over the edge of the cliff, falling away from them in a steep slope down to the road below.

"That's the East River Drive," Tilo said. "You can hear the cars. It's right on the edge of the Schuylkill River."

"Okay." Diggy turned and looked out over the lawn. He shook his head. "Some house, huh?"

"Like something out of a nightmare," Bobbie said.

"Any idea where you'd bury a treasure around here if you were in a treasure-burying mood?" Sphinx asked.

Larry shook his head. "Don't know. I sure hope she didn't bury it somewhere in these woods. If it's on the side of this cliff, we'll never find it."

Chessie was looking at the outcropping of rock at the edge of the woods. "I'd bury it here. Those rock formations are incredible."

"I'd bury it nearer the house," Bobbie said. "It's even spookier than out here."

"Well, okay," Diggy said. "We have a general idea what this looks like now. No clues as to where the treasure might be—yet. There's the house and the lawn, which runs to these woods. This cliff goes down to the road and the river. All right. Enough work for one day. And Sphinx, don't sweat it, okay? You're going to get your clue, don't worry."

"Who's worried?" Sphinx said miserably.

□

That night Sphinx prepared to wage a final battle against Joyce Henning and her clue.

He went into his room after dinner, dumped his books on the bed, got out a fresh pad of paper, and sat down at the desk. He sharpened a pencil and put it down neatly by the pad. Then he threw away the pile of scrap paper which contained all his scribblings to date, all the scrawled numbers and question marks. He took out *Dragonstone*. He turned to Clue Number Seven and tried to read it as if he had never seen it before.

17163034546267
12025395968828799
12040556974

Okay, he thought. *Dr. Henning claims these clues aren't hard if you know how to look at them. I'll bet that means all this complicated stuff I've been doing is the wrong way to go about it. It must be some kind of one-step process, from this code to the answer. At most, two steps. Not the endless code-from-a-code method I've been trying.*

What one step could you take from these numbers that would generate a meaningful answer?

He chewed the pencil eraser reflectively. He had already tried dividing the numbers up into pairs. He decided to look at that again.

```
17 16 30 34 54 62 67
12 02 53 95 96 88 28 79 9
12 04 05 56 97 4
```

That was okay, except the *9* and the *4* at the ends looked kind of funny. Now, what if you added the columns up and multiplied the totals by—

He stopped himself. Something *simple*, he thought grimly. Nothing too fancy.

The numbers went outside the range of the alphabet—26—fairly quickly. Maybe taking the differences between every two neighboring numbers would make them fit. He tried it.

```
1 14 4 20 8 5
10 51 42 1 8 60 51 70
8 1 51 41 93
```

He could see it was wrong from the numbers in the last two lines, which were too large to refer to the alphabet. Still, he doggedly began replacing the numbers with letters wherever possible. *1* was *A, 14* was *N* . . .

```
A N D T H E
J _ _ A H _ _ _   ·
H A _ _ _
```

He squinted at the answer. The first line looked like something. He surveyed the paired numbers again.

What one step would generate a meaningful sequence? he asked himself. What *one step* . . .

He looked back at the original clue. Now, the funny thing was that if you looked at it the right way, the numbers seemed to form an ascending sequence, particularly toward the end of each line. What if you divided them up so that . . .

Hmmm. His pencil flew over the paper.

```
1 7 16 30 34 54 62 67
1 20 25 39 59 68 82 87 99
1 20 40 55 69 74
```

Okay. There were the ascending sequences. They each started with *1* and went above the 26 limit of the alphabet. But if you subtracted each number from the next . . .

```
6 9 14 4 20 8 5
19 5 14 20 9 14 5 12
19 20 15 14 5
```

Sphinx stared at the numbers for a long moment, then began to pound his fist on the desk. He leaned back in his chair and shook his head.

"Easy?" he said out loud. "And she calls that *easy?!"*

6

□ Sphinx galloped into homeroom the next day, a smug expression on his face.

"I'd like you to see something," he said to Bobbie.

"Okay, what is it?"

"Nothing much," Sphinx said. "Look." He slid a piece of paper onto her desk.

On it, in Sphinx's uneven handwriting, were the numbers,

6 9 14 4 20 8 5
19 5 14 20 9 14 5 12
19 20 15 14 5

and underneath that,

F I N D T H E
S E N T I N E L
S T O N E

Bobbie glanced quickly from the words back to the code. "Oh, Sphinx," she breathed. "Congratulations!"

"They thought it wasn't possible," Sphinx said, his old cocky self again. "The world laughed. But to everyone's amazement he went ahead and did it anyway."

"What in the world is the Sentinel Stone?"

"Beats me. What does it matter? I solved the clue. I can show my face in public again. I can go out of my house in daylight." Sphinx crumpled up a piece of paper and tossed it across the room. "I may, someday, actually do homework again."

"It's got to be near the Riverhill Mansion," Bobbie said to herself. "In that rock outcropping. We'll have to go back there and take a look around."

"Look at Clue Number Eight," Sphinx said. "The shadow it talks about must be cast by this stone."

"Uh-huh." Bobbie looked up at him, her eyes bright. "You know, we're really getting somewhere now."

"You don't have to tell me," Sphinx said, strolling jauntily to his desk. "I spent all last evening telling myself how wonderful I was."

□

The gang stood in front of the Riverhill Mansion again. The grounds stretched out all around them. They could see the cliff which dropped off to the road and the Schuylkill River far below. Tilo held up the book and read out loud.

" 'Clue Number Eight: When the eye watches you

from the sky/And night is all around,/ Pace out from where the shadow starts/And dig there in the ground. The number of paces is twice the hour, three times the depth in feet, and equal to the month. If you count to ten, you'll have named them all.' Whew!"

"I've figured it out," Bobbie announced smugly. "Six paces. Three o'clock. Two feet down. In June."

They turned to her in astonishment.

"Those are the only numbers that fit the clue and that are between one and ten," Bobbie explained. "Six, three, two, six. The sixth month is June. It wasn't that hard. I've been looking at that clue for a while."

"It's November now," said Chessie.

"Yes," said Diggy. "We'll have to calculate backward to last June to know where that shadow would have been. But right now, does anyone see anything that looks like it might be a sentinel stone?"

They circled slowly about. "There," Chessie said, pointing. "Over there. That big rock."

About twenty yards away from them, across the lawn, a long narrow rock which pointed like a needle toward the sky jutted out from the outcropping in front of the cliff. The thin shadow it cast in the sunlight lay across the lawn. They gathered around it and stared upward.

"This must be it," Diggy said. "Okay. The treasure was buried last June, on the night of the full moon— at least I guess that's what 'when the eye watches you' means, a full moon. The shadow from this rock at three A.M. was her guide. She walked six paces from the rock along the line of the shadow. It's going to be complicated, but we'll have to duplicate those conditions. When's the next full moon?"

"In a couple days," Sphinx replied. "I know because I usually go outside and howl at it."

"If we're going to calculate where the shadow was in June," Larry said, "we don't have to wait for the full moon this month, do we?"

"No, but it'll be easier with more light. I don't want to be out here in the middle of the night with no moon at all—do you?" Diggy said.

Larry looked back at the spooky, medieval-looking house. "No, I guess not."

"Okay. Sphinx, how hard do you think this calculation is going to be?" Diggy asked.

"It's not going to be easy," Sphinx replied thoughtfully. "To figure out the direction of the shadow at a certain hour on a certain day of the year . . . I don't know. Hold on." He brightened. "I can call the Franklin Institute. Someone there should be able to help me with the calculations."

"All right." Diggy started to leave, the others trailing after him.

"It's strange," Bobbie said, glancing around, "to know that the ring might be buried right around here, isn't it?"

"Yeah," said Chessie, bundled up in her jacket. "I'm really looking forward to coming out here in the middle of the night too."

"Mmm-hmm." Bobbie nodded.

"We'll come back out here as soon as you've called the institute," Diggy was saying to Sphinx as they rounded the corner of the mansion.

"Okay, I'll call as soon as—" Sphinx said and suddenly stopped. There in front of them was a man, leaning against the wall of the building and gazing out over the front lawn. He turned when the gang came around the corner, and walked away.

"Do you think he's here for the same reason we are?" Chessie asked in a whisper.

"Could be just a tourist," Tilo said.

"No, look!" Bobbie said, pointing. A copy of *Dragonstone* was sticking out of the man's coat pocket.

"Oh, no, that means he's figured it out this far," Chessie said with a groan.

Diggy shrugged, taking her arm. "Well, we knew that might happen. Come on. There aren't exactly hordes of people around here yet, are there?"

"It's not three A.M. yet either," Sphinx said, looking around nervously. "Let's hope we don't have to elbow for room then."

□

The next day Sphinx got up early and called the Franklin Institute. The information desk transferred his call to the planetarium, and from there to the office of Dr. Lethgow, a staff astronomer. The phone rang several times before it was picked up.

"Lethgow here." The voice was female and sounded young.

"Dr. Lethgow, my name is Oliver Osgood"—

68

Sphinx winced; he hated his real name and any occasion on which he was forced to use it—"and I have an astronomy question which I need some help on."

"Yes, go right ahead."

"It has to do with calculating the position of the full moon last June."

There was a startled pause. "Why is everyone so interested in the full moon last June?" she asked. "This must be the fifth query I've received about this problem. Is there something I don't know?"

"The fifth?" Sphinx faltered. *Oh, no,* he thought. *Someone's been here before us.*

"That's right."

"Well, it has to do with the book *Dragonstone,* by Joyce Henning. Have you heard about it? In order to solve the last clue, you have to make certain calculations—"

"Oh, I get it." The astronomer laughed. "Okay, that explains the sudden interest in astronomy. I guess I should have tried it myself. All right, young man, let me show you how to solve this problem. You can calculate the shift in the moon's angle in the following way. . . ."

□

When Sphinx hung up, he thought for a while, looking over his page of notes and drumming his pencil on the table. Then he called Diggy and briefly explained what the astronomer had said.

". . . I think I can do it," he finished. "I'll need some time to make the calculations and check all the figures. She wished me good luck when she hung up. We'll need it. Diggy, there have already been at least four other calls about this."

"Doesn't mean anything," Diggy said. "People could've figured out the last clue and nothing else."

"Still, we'd better hurry. I told the astronomer we'd be there tonight at three A.M."

"Okay, fine. It's not quite a full moon, but there'll be enough light. And it's Saturday, so we can sleep late tomorrow."

"Call the others and tell them to meet us at the bus stop. We'll take the last bus out there."

"Okay. See you later, Sphinx."

"Wish me luck!"

□

An hour later Sphinx double-checked his figures for the last time. Then he put on his jacket and went for a walk. He decided to head north toward his school. He might shoot a few baskets if there was a game going.

Halfway there he stopped. Across the street from him, sitting on a bench, were the four kids who had challenged them in midtown a few days ago. Their voices were raised.

"No, Pete, that's not right," one of them was saying in exasperation. He was holding a book in his hand. "Look here, it says—" He stopped suddenly as one of the other boys grabbed his arm and pointed at Sphinx.

The one named Pete got up from the bench and

crossed the street. He was the same one who had talked to the Galaxy Gang earlier.

"Hi," he said. He stuck out his hand. He was taller than Sphinx and more strongly built.

"Hi," said Sphinx. He slowly put out his hand.

"Listen," said Pete, "I'm sorry about what I said the other day. I got carried away, I guess. I had no right to warn you guys off. The more competition, the better."

"Okay," Sphinx said uncomfortably. "I'll tell the others."

"Good." The boy seemed to relax. "Had any luck with the clues?"

Sphinx shrugged. "Not really."

"Oh. I thought maybe we could help each other out. You know, trade clues."

"I don't think so." Sphinx began to back away.

"C'mon, tell me," Pete persisted. "Any luck with 'a house on hill'? Do you know which one she means? I'll trade you one of the other clues for that."

Sphinx decided to put an end to this. His face slowly brightened. "A house on hill?" he repeated. "Wow, is that one of the answers? We didn't have that one! Thanks a lot. Do you have any of the other—"

Pete glared at him. "Oh, shut up," he snapped. He turned and walked back toward his friends. "If you don't want to trade, then just say so!"

"You're sure you don't have any of the others?" Sphinx called after him. "C'mon, you can tell me! We don't have number five yet either."

"Forget it!" Pete called from the other side of the street. "Forget the whole thing!"

"Glad to," Sphinx said and strolled away.

□

"They're on to us," he told Diggy and Chessie at midnight when they met at the bus stop. The last bus for Fairmount Park would be along in a few minutes. "They know something. We'd better be extra careful what we say, where we go. Pete said they don't know about Riverhill Mansion yet, but he could've been lying about that."

Diggy shrugged. "Last time they tried to scare us," he said. "This time this guy Pete tried to sweet-talk you into an exchange. Big deal. I bet they're not even close."

"I wouldn't count on that," Sphinx said. "They've probably been getting answers from everybody they meet who's on the treasure hunt. And Pete isn't stupid."

"We'll be careful," Chessie said, her voice half-muffled by her scarf. "I'm less worried about that other gang than I am about our freezing to death out there tonight. Or about my parents finding out where I am. It wasn't easy to sneak out of the house." She looked up at the sky. "At least it's a clear night."

"Not to worry," Larry said. He had just walked up, carrying a large boxlike object in one hand and a shovel in the other. He lifted the box so everyone could see. "It's a portable battery-run heater," he said. "We'll be warm once we get there, I promise."

Bobbie and Tilo joined them in a few minutes. They were both carrying shovels. The bus came shortly afterward. The gang got on, laughing and chattering.

"It's empty," Chessie said, looking at the rows of vacant seats.

"I'm not surprised," Bobbie replied. "Who else is this crazy?"

"Who else is going to be this rich?" Sphinx asked confidently, leaning back against his seat.

"You really think we're going to find the dragon ring, huh, Sphinx?" Larry asked.

"Absolutely." Sphinx waved a notebook in the air. "The answer's in here. If I've done it right—and I promise you I have—we'll have the treasure in our hands by three A.M."

Bobbie sighed. "I just hope you're right about this, Sphinx," she said. "I'm going to be awfully mad if I stay out all night in Fairmount Park for nothing."

"You can say that again," Larry said grimly, looking out the window as they rumbled through the city streets.

The bus let them off, as before, on the edge of the park. They took out their flashlights and began to walk.

"Where are we?" Tilo asked. "This doesn't look familiar."

"No lights or anything," Chessie said.

"Don't worry," replied Diggy. "Riverhill Mansion is right up there. Just over that rise."

They toiled up the hill in the darkness, the beams

from their flashlights wavering. When they topped the rise, they could see the outline of Riverhill Mansion, sharp-edged in the moonlight. Sphinx grunted in satisfaction. "The Sentinel Stone is right over there."

They hurried across the lawn, grouped together in a tight knot. The lawn was bathed in moonlight. They reached the stone and looked at the long shadow it cast in the pale, watery light.

Larry put the heater on the ground and flicked it on. "C'mon, everybody. This thing isn't very strong, so we'll have to stay close to it."

They gathered in a small circle and sat warming their hands. Nobody said anything. The scene, lit by moonlight, with the Gothic mass of Riverhill Mansion towering in the background, was eerie and frightening. Far below they could hear the sound of cars, but other than that everything around them was still. The lights of the city twinkled in the distance.

Sphinx was busy with a yardstick he had unfolded, a small stake, a ball of string, and his notebook. He knelt on the grass by the shadow of the Sentinel Stone, muttering to himself.

The time crept by. Chessie grew sleepy. She was wearing two heavy sweaters, a wool coat, mittens, and a scarf, and that combined with the warmth of the heater made her feel comfortably drowsy. Her head nodded, and she fell asleep on Diggy's shoulder.

The others were all half-asleep as well. They huddled around the heater, their heads nodding. At last Sphinx stood up and came over to join them.

"Not much longer now," he said, sitting down beside Diggy.

There was no answer.

"Diggy," Sphinx said a little louder; still no reply. He glanced around the circle and shook his head. "Watch out! We're being attacked by aliens from the planet Zorn!" he announced.

Larry shook his head in his sleep and mumbled.

"The cliff is collapsing, and the Sentinel Stone is about to fall on us!" Sphinx said next.

Silence.

Sphinx sighed and warmed his hands over the heater. "It's just lucky I wasn't counting on you guys to be my bodyguards," he said.

□

Half an hour later they were awakened by Sphinx, who shook their shoulders roughly. "It's a miracle one of us had the sense to stay awake," he said, shining his flashlight on his watch to check the time. "What if we had slept past three o'clock, hmmm?"

Diggy scrambled to his feet. "What time's it?" he mumbled.

"Don't worry, it's just about time now. Come on," Sphinx replied.

They gathered near the shadow of the Sentinel Stone. Sphinx had his eyes on his watch and the stake in his hand. "All right, everybody," he said. "I have fifteen seconds to go. Chessie? Tilo? Everybody check their watch."

They counted down, chanting the last five seconds. "Five—four—three—two—one—*now!*"

With the stake, Sphinx rapidly scratched the ground along the thin line of the shadow. Then he placed the yardstick against the base of the Sentinel Stone, and measured along the shadow line. He made a mark in the ground and turned the yardstick so that it lay against the mark at right angles to the shadow.

He measured carefully along the yardstick, made another mark, and put the stake in the ground there. Taking the ball of string out of his pocket, he tied one end around the stake. Then, playing the string out through his hands, he backed up until he stood against the Sentinel Stone.

"Chessie," he said, "come here and hold this string, okay?"

She ran over and held it taut a few inches from the ground at the base of the stone. Sphinx stepped forward along the line of the string for six paces. He stopped and stamped his foot on the ground.

"Right here," he said. "It should be right here."

"How do we know that your paces are accurate enough, Sphinx?" Bobbie asked.

"We don't," he replied. "We'll have to dig a wide enough hole. It should be right around here, though. Joyce Henning's paces couldn't have been that different."

"Okay," Diggy said. "Tilo, Larry, let's start digging. The others can take over when we get tired."

The ground was hard at this time of year, and they were tired, so it took a long time and a lot of bickering. Chessie, Bobbie, and Sphinx relieved the first three after a while. They worked in shifts, back and forth.

"Whew," groaned Larry, leaning on his shovel. "Two feet down is harder than I thought. Aren't we there yet?"

"Keep going," Diggy said, fatigue in his voice. "It's about a foot and a half now."

"Sixteen inches," Sphinx said, measuring the depth with the yardstick.

Bobbie stood nearby. Her heart was pounding. Could it be that they were really only a few inches away from the buried treasure? She glanced at Chessie. Chessie's face was shining, and she smiled back at Bobbie. "Almost there!" she said.

The boys caught the excitement as they got closer. They swung their shovels harder, the sound of their breathing loud in the semidarkness. Sphinx had his flashlight focused on the bottom of the hole.

"We should see it soon," he said.

A minute passed. Another. Diggy pressed into his work willingly, as did Larry and Tilo. The dirt flew. Sphinx kept the flashlight beam sweeping the bottom of the hole. A puzzled expression crept over his face.

Another minute passed. Diggy stopped, gasping for breath. "Hey, Sphinx, aren't we there yet?"

The other two stopped, leaning on their shovels.

Sphinx lowered the yardstick into the ground.

"Yeah," he said. "Twenty-six inches. We're past it already."

Oh, no, Bobbie thought. Aloud she said, "Maybe

Sphinx's paces were a little off. Why don't we try digging around that spot?"

The boys nodded.

"Okay, guys," Diggy said. "Bobbie's right. Tilo, you dig there." He indicated one edge of the hole. "Larry, you start there, and I'll work on this part."

Chessie's face was grim, and her eyes were on Sphinx.

The boys' breathing sounded labored, and in spite of the cold night sweat stood out on their faces. Larry straightened up with a grunt and took off his jacket.

They dug for a while, widening the hole in the ground along the line of the string, but they found— nothing. Sphinx stood over them, his expression growing slowly sadder and sadder. Finally Bobbie jerked her head toward Chessie.

"C'mon," she said. "Let's take over for a while."

Diggy and the other two gratefully let go of their shovels as Sphinx, Bobbie, and Chessie bent to the work. It was backbreaking. Bobbie clenched her teeth as she shoveled dirt into the air. *If Sphinx was wrong . . .*

A sudden thought brought her up sharply. It didn't have to be Sphinx. Any of them could have made a mistake. They could be digging miles from the real spot of the buried treasure.

Chessie was heartily wishing that she was home and sound asleep. She dug her shovel furiously into the ground, stamping on it with her foot.

Sphinx was ready to shoot himself. All this work, all this trouble, and for what? He had brought them all out here in the middle of the night on a wild goose chase. He felt worse than he ever had in his whole life. He had this terrible dead feeling that they weren't going to find anything, anything at all. It had all been for nothing.

Fifteen minutes later they gave up. The hole was wide enough and deep enough to account for any inaccuracies, if the overall idea was right. Sphinx leaned on his shovel and felt like crying.

"All right," he said, although no one had said anything. "I'll kill myself, okay? Just to make up for this."

Bobbie took his arm. "Don't be stupid, Sphinx," she said. "Nobody blames you. It could've been any of us."

Sphinx shook his head. "What went wrong?" he mumbled. "What went wrong? I did the calculations so *carefully*. . . ."

"Never mind about that now." Bobbie spoke soothingly. "Listen, I think we'd better fill up this hole again. Visitors to Riverhill Mansion aren't going to enjoy finding holes all over the property. And we'd better get going." She looked at her watch. "It's nearly four o'clock."

Diggy, Chessie, and Tilo began to fill up the hole. Larry put on his jacket, then went over and switched off the heater. Sphinx stood slumped over the shovel.

"What did I do wrong?" he asked Bobbie. "Really, I was so careful about not making a mistake."

"I know," Bobbie said. She patted his shoulder. "You did the best you could, Sphinx. We'll talk about it tomorrow, okay? Right now we have to get home and get some sleep."

Sphinx shook his head.

Ten minutes later they stumbled out of the park and stood in a small knot by the side of the road leading to town. The bus came shortly afterward—"Lucky," Larry said as they got on board—and they were home and asleep within the hour. Before they separated at the bus stop, Diggy gave them strict instructions to meet at his house at five o'clock that afternoon.

"We'll talk this over," he said.

"Take care of him, okay?" Bobbie said as Diggy led Sphinx away toward their apartment house.

"I'll get him home safe and sound," Diggy said. "See you later on today."

"Don't talk about it," Tilo said tiredly. "Chessie, let's go."

"Okay. See everybody later!"

7

☐ "It's not anyone's fault, Sphinx," Diggy said. The gang was gathered in the living room of his apartment. "Honestly."

"Yes, it is," Sphinx replied. "It's my fault. Stop being so nice about it."

"Any of us could've made a mistake," Tilo put in. He was thumbing through his copy of *Dragonstone*. "We could have one of these clues all wrong."

"Maybe it's not at Riverhill Mansion at all," Larry said.

Sphinx groaned. "It's my mistake, okay? Everybody please stop trying to make me feel better. I'm going to have to figure out by myself what went wrong."

"I know everybody's tired—" Diggy began. He was met by a chorus of groans.

"You can say that again," Chessie complained. "I

snuck in the back way and almost knocked over all the garbage cans. I just knew that monster Frankie would be waiting for me at the top of the stairs, ready to tell my folks how late I'd been out. He was sound asleep, though—the way I wish *I* had been."

"I had to get up at ten o'clock so my parents wouldn't be suspicious," Larry said.

"My parents had some friends over for brunch, and I had to be pleasant to them," said Bobbie. "I'm tired of smiling."

"Still, I want everyone to go home and try to figure out where we went wrong," Diggy said. "Check your clue, check everybody else's clues. Do your best. I know we're close—I can feel it."

There were a few tired moans, but everyone nodded.

"Okay," Diggy said. "Get moving. We'll talk over any ideas we come up with tomorrow in school. Sphinx, stop blaming yourself. Just go home and double-check your calculations."

"It's a lot easier to keep on blaming myself," Sphinx said.

□

Sphinx and Bobbie went out for a walk after the meeting. They were strolling through Society Hill, stopping every now and then to look in shop windows, when Sphinx grabbed her arm.

"Look," he whispered. "There are those kids—the ones who threatened us before."

Pete and his friends were coming down the street toward them.

"They must live in this neighborhood," Bobbie said. "Let's get out of here."

"They've seen us already," Sphinx said. "C'mon. We'll bluff them."

"Well, if it isn't Red and his girl friend," Pete called as they got closer. "How're you doing?"

"Fine," said Sphinx.

"Listen, tell your friends you haven't got a chance of beating us now," Pete said. "We know where the treasure is buried."

Sphinx tried to brush past them, but Bobbie stopped, planted her feet on the sidewalk, and put her hands on her hips. "Really? That's strange," she said.

"Strange? What's so strange about it?" said Pete.

"Didn't you read the paper today?" she asked. "The dragon ring was just found. It's all over the front page. Or perhaps," she asked witheringly, "you can't read?"

Pete and his friends had turned white.

"It's been found?" one of them asked hoarsely.

Bobbie nodded. "All over the front page," she said. "Why don't you take a look?"

Pete turned and fled, followed by his buddies. Sphinx gave Bobbie a look of admiration.

"You've got a real talent," he said. "I never knew you could lie like that."

Bobbie linked arms with him. "I'd never have reached such an advanced age if I couldn't. Those idiots," she added. "They couldn't possibly have found it. They don't have one working brain between them."

"No, but they're great at picking everyone else's," Sphinx said, laughing. "I'm not worried—yet. Seems to me that if we can't solve the clues, those guys don't have a chance."

"That's the spirit, Sphinx."

□

The next few days were uneventful. Each of them went over his or her clue and the solution, but they could find nothing wrong. Sphinx went over his calculations ten times but always came up with the same answer. His face grew longer and longer, and he began to mope visibly around the school.

"Cheer up," Bobbie told him.

"I can't. What if those guys get it before we do?"

"You mean Pete and his friends?"

Sphinx nodded.

"Well, we would've heard about it by now if they'd found it. They were just bluffing us, Sphinx, the way we've been bluffing them. Don't worry so much."

"I can't help it. I'm a worrier. I get it from my mother."

After school that day Bobbie made Sphinx sit down and show her his calculations. When he was done, she sat silently for a long time.

"I don't know, Sphinx," she said at last. "It looks all right to me. I can't see where you've made a mistake. But there's something about it that just doesn't feel right."

"Doesn't feel right?"

"Yeah." Bobbie brushed her hair impatiently away from her face. "I can't put my finger on it. I just feel that there's something wrong somewhere."

"Well, that's for sure." Sphinx stared morosely down at the paper. "I don't know what it could be, though. I've been over these figures a hundred times."

Bobbie nodded. "Let me think about it a bit," she suggested. "It may come to me later."

"Sure, take your time," Sphinx replied, gathering up the sheaf of papers. "I'm going nowhere fast."

☐

The next day after school Sphinx felt so depressed that he went down to visit Diggy, who lived in the same apartment house. When Sphinx came back, his mother handed him a slip of paper.

"Bobbie called," she said. "She asked me to write this down and give it to you. She said you'd understand." Mrs. Osgood gave her son a sharp look. "Another one of your schemes?"

Sphinx did not reply. He was staring at the note in his hand, a look of shock on his face. There were three words written on the slip of paper.

"What is it?" his mother asked.

Sphinx shook his head slowly. He ran his fingers through his hair until it all stood on end. "Nothing," he said. "Nothing. I'm shocked at my own stupidity, that's all. Though by this time I guess I shouldn't even be surprised."

He picked up the phone, ran into his bedroom and slammed the door.

Mrs. Osgood regarded the door thoughtfully. "Children!" she said to herself.

In his bedroom Sphinx sat down at his desk and dialled the number of the Franklin Institute. After a short conversation with Dr. Lethgow, he pulled his notebook toward him and worked feverishly for half an hour. Then he stood up, stretched, and glanced over his figures again.

That should do it.

He grabbed the note from Bobbie and left the apartment, hurriedly calling to his mother that he'd be back soon.

Diggy opened his front door and stared at Sphinx, who stood wild-eyed, hair bristling, in the hallway.

"Correct me if I'm wrong," Diggy said, "but didn't you just leave here a little while ago?"

"I solved it!" Sphinx cried, pushing past him into the apartment. "I solved it! Or rather, Bobbie solved it. She figured out where my mistake was."

"You're kidding!" Diggy followed him into the dining room, where Sphinx sat down and shoved the slip of paper toward him.

"It's so simple," Sphinx said. "Such an obvious mistake!"

On the note were scrawled three words: *Daylight Saving Time.*

"Daylight Saving Time?" Diggy said.

"Of course. Three A.M. in June isn't three A.M. in

November, it's *two* A.M.! My calculations were all off by an hour." Sphinx gazed morosely at the table.

"Bobbie thought of this?"

"Uh-huh. She told me yesterday, when I showed her my calculations, that something 'felt' wrong about it. She was right. It's not a big difference, but it's enough to throw us off."

"We have to get out there quick, Sphinx," Diggy said, his voice strained. "Somebody else could have figured this out by now."

"You can say that again."

"How about tonight?"

Sphinx nodded. "I hope everyone else can make it. I called the astronomer and recalculated everything for tonight—at *two* A.M."

"We have school tomorrow."

"Who cares? I'm flunking out anyway this term."

"I'll call Chessie and Larry. You call Bobbie and Tilo. And thank Bobbie for all of us. She hit the nail on the head."

"I know. I'm tempted to give her a bigger cut in the prize money, except then there'd be less for me."

"You're generous to a fault, as always, Sphinx."

☐

There were a lot of grumbles and complaints at the bus stop that night. The six of them met at midnight. When the bus came, Bobbie sank into a seat and pressed her nose to the window.

"I don't believe I'm doing this again," she said with a sigh.

"Tell me about it," Chessie said. "I feel like I'm in the Twilight Zone."

"We're crazy," Larry said. "All of us. Completely crazy."

Tilo said nothing. He was not a complainer. He sat quietly, looking doleful.

Only Sphinx was optimistic. "We have it this time," he crowed. "Believe me! I can see that seventy-five thousand dollars already. What are you going to do with your share, Chessie?"

"Sphinx, shut up."

"How about you?" he asked Bobbie, undaunted.

"I'm going to take a nice long vacation," she said. "I'm going to need it after this."

"How about you, Larry?"

"I don't know. I haven't wasted much time thinking about it, Sphinx. I'll probably get a new stereo, and then put the rest away for college."

"Boring," Sphinx decided.

"Well, it may be boring, but it's practical, which is more than I can say for your ideas," Larry replied.

Tilo spoke up. "I'd buy an arcade game," he said, his eyes sparkling. "I'd buy one of the newest games and take it home and have it there whenever I wanted to play it."

"Now *that's* what I call thinking," said Sphinx.

"I'd buy my own computer," Larry said. "Yeah."

"Too late," Sphinx said. "Tilo got in first with the video game. Not a computer game, but the real thing. We'll all be over at Tilo's house if you want us, Larry."

"This is our stop," Diggy said, and they ran to the front of the bus. They clambered down the steps and took out their flashlights.

"It's twelve thirty A.M.," Diggy said. "Okay. That way. Let's go."

They toiled up the hill again and saw the lawn spreading out before them in the wavering beams of their flashlights. The Sentinel Stone was silhouetted against the sky. The night was slightly cloudy, with a touch of wind.

"Not much moon tonight," Bobbie said.

"It'll be okay," Sphinx said, "as long as it doesn't get any worse."

They walked across the lawn. As they drew closer to the stone Chessie let out an exclamation of surprise. "Look!"

They ran forward. There in front of them was the hole that they had filled up—freshly redug! And around it on the lawn were four other holes, nearly as large as the first. Diggy turned over some of the soil with his foot.

"So now we know," he said. "Sphinx, do you think whoever it is found the ring?"

Sphinx was prowling around the other holes. He squinted up at the moon, now clear through the scudding clouds.

"Naaah," he said irritably. "They don't have the right direction. They were just digging at random."

"Was this the hole we dug last time?" Diggy asked.

"Yes," said Larry. He judged the distance from the stone. "Looks like somebody came out here, saw where that hole had been, and tried it again along with all these others."

"Well, they didn't get it, so let's forget about it," Diggy said briskly. "Larry, set up the heater. We have a wait ahead of us."

"At least it's not as long as the other night," Bobbie said, crouching down by the heater as Larry flicked it on.

"We can sing campfire songs," Sphinx suggested.

"I can't stand his good humor, can you?" Larry asked Tilo. "I like it better when he's depressed."

"We've got it now," Sphinx was saying to Chessie. "I can feel it. It's right around here somewhere. We may be standing right on top of it, for all we know."

"Yes, Sphinx, and a big wind might come along and carry us all off to Oz," Chessie said.

"Disbeliever!" Sphinx replied in shocked tones.

"I don't blame her after the other night," Bobbie said.

"Heretic!" said Sphinx. "O ye of little faith!" He glanced up at the sky and checked his watch. "If the moon doesn't come out again soon, we'll be in trouble. Come on, baby, you can do it!" he called at the sky.

"*Shhhhh,*" said Diggy. "We don't want anybody to know we're here."

"Who's going to know—the squirrels?" Larry said.

"Maybe the person who dug these holes will come back," Tilo said uneasily.

"Well, let's hope not. But let's keep our voices down," Diggy said.

Larry unpacked the bag he was carrying. "Here's some stuff I brought along in case we got hungry. Sandwiches for everyone."

It was a long wait. The hour seemed to drag by. They talked in low voices, keeping an anxious eye on the moon, and watched the shadow of the Sentinel Stone creep over the ground. At quarter of two Sphinx stood up, stretched, and took out a ball of string.

"Okay, Chessie," he said. "Here we go again."

He took out his notebook and glanced up at the moon. "Where's my yardstick and stake?" He fumbled in his knapsack. "Here we go. Now we just wait until two o'clock on the dot and pray the moon is out."

"I'm getting this terrible sense that we've been through this before," Bobbie whispered to Larry.

They shone their flashlights on their watches and sat silently, waiting. The minutes ticked by.

They chorused, *"Now!"*

The moon was behind a cloud. Sphinx stared at the sky, a scowl on his face. "Come on, baby," he muttered.

The cloud moved slowly past. The pale milky light touched the tip of the Sentinel Stone, throwing a faint shadow across the lawn.

"There!" cried Sphinx and pounced on it. He made a scratch on the ground along the line of the shadow, and then rapidly repeated the procedure he had followed the last time. He measured from the Sentinel Stone along the shadow line, made a mark, measured from that mark at right angles to the shadow, and made another mark. He stuck the stake in the ground at that point, and tied the string around it. Backing off until he stood against the stone, he said, "Chessie, will you hold this for me?"

Chessie took the string. "I'm getting good at this," she remarked.

Starting with his back to the stone, Sphinx paced off six steps along the line of the string. He leaned down and put a pebble on the spot.

"Here," he said firmly, pointing. "Right here. Two feet down."

Diggy motioned to the others. "Bobbie, Tilo, come on. Larry, you and Chessie and Sphinx can take over for us later."

Bobbie had been tired, but as she started to dig the adrenaline flooded her body, and she found herself getting more and more enthusiastic. The pile of dirt beside them mounted. The others gathered closely around to watch. Could it be that they were actually going to unearth the treasure?

Chessie was shivering with cold and anticipation. She pulled the heater closer to the hole. The three who weren't digging kept their flashlights focused on the inside of the hole.

Sphinx's face was impassive as he watched. He was fighting a wave of fear. *What if he was wrong again?*

"Whew!" said Diggy, leaning on his shovel. "That's enough. You guys take over."

The ground was hard, and as before, it took several

shifts before the hole seemed deep enough. Sphinx lowered the yardstick.

"Not quite," he said, trying to keep his voice calm. "An inch and a half more."

"Okay," said Bobbie.

Chessie found she was holding her breath. She huddled on the ground near the hole, her flashlight fixed on the bottom. Suddenly she let out a cry.

"There's something there!" she said.

Diggy's spade had hit something which didn't feel like earth. He knelt down, leaned into the hole, and began to scrabble with his hands.

"She's right," he told the others, his voice tight. "There's something—feels like metal or something." He tapped it with his knuckles, and there was a dull ring. "It's hollow." He scrambled to his feet. "Keep digging," he said. "We have to clear a space around it."

Sphinx grabbed the spade from Tilo, and Chessie took Bobbie's. They bent to work with a will and quickly opened up the hole, making it wider at the bottom.

"That's enough now," Diggy ordered. He reached down and felt around the metal until he found an edge. He slid his hand underneath and shook the dirt loose.

"Here we go." He reached in with his other hand and carefully lifted the object out.

They gathered around silently. It was a metal box about nine inches long and three inches deep. It was inlaid with strange flowing letters, flowers, and trees in silver and gold. The top was fastened with a small clasp.

"So open it already," Sphinx said hoarsely.

Diggy touched the clasp. It opened easily. He lifted the top and swung it back.

Inside was a piece of parchment, yellow and curled. Diggy lifted it, his hand trembling. Underneath was a smaller box made of red velvet.

On the parchment was written, in golden ink,

Hail, Adventurer: The Treasure Is Thine.

Diggy read it out loud and passed it around. Then he held up the velvet box and opened it slowly.

There, mounted on plush red velvet, was the dragon ring. Diggy took it out and lifted it between his fingers. It was cunningly made. The dragon's mouth was bared as if to roar, its body was curled in a circle to form the ring, and its tail was looped to form a base for the large diamond which sparkled brilliantly in front of the dragon's emerald eyes. The ring was etched with tiny designs, and the dragon's body was inset with smooth sapphires. Diggy turned the box so the others could see. He was speechless.

He heard Chessie gasp. "It's so beautiful," she murmured.

Bobbie grabbed Tilo's arm. "Can you believe it?"

"Will you look at that," Larry said, his voice hushed.

For once in his life Sphinx could think of nothing to say.

They were standing there, staring at the ring,

when there was a sudden rustling and crackling in the bushes nearby.

There was a pounding of feet, and Chessie screamed. Diggy did not have time to move before he was knocked to the ground and the ring was snatched out of his hand. Tilo yelled something, but he and Sphinx were knocked aside, their flashlights flying from their hands.

They could hear the sound of footsteps disappearing into the woods near the cliff. Chessie, Bobbie, and Larry swept the woods with their flashlights.

"There!" cried Bobbie. The beams revealed several shapes running through the trees.

"Come on!" shouted Diggy, struggling to his feet. "After them! They've got the ring!"

Tilo and Sphinx grabbed their flashlights, then pelted after the others.

Diggy was first. He ran into the woods, sweeping his flashlight back and forth. Ahead of him he could hear the crackling of twigs underfoot. "This way!" he called.

He was gaining on the sound of footsteps when suddenly the ground gave way beneath him, and he found himself rolling down the side of the hill!

He fell almost fifty feet before he slammed into a tree. He climbed to his feet, gasping. His flashlight was broken, and with a sound of disgust he threw it away.

"Careful!" he shouted back to his friends. "Be careful of the hill!"

He could hear the rest of the gang scrambling

down the path behind him. "We're okay!" came back Sphinx's answering shout.

Diggy turned and plunged again into the undergrowth.

He was scratched and bruised when he finally broke free of the woods. Directly in front of him was the River Drive, illuminated by streetlights. One lone figure was running across the road.

A car swung around the curve, its headlights nearly blinding him. Diggy shrank back instinctively behind a tree until it passed. Then he raced across the road in pursuit.

The gang appeared at the edge of the woods. They ran toward him, but their path was blocked as three cars came around the curve. Diggy could hear Sphinx's howl of frustration.

The dark figure in front of him was lengthening the distance between them when all at once it stopped, looked around, and scuttled off to the left.

Diggy forced his unwilling legs to move faster. The blood was pounding in his ears, and his whole body ached from the fall down the hill. He turned left, ran through a line of bushes, and found himself next to the river. There was a boathouse to his right, illuminated by strings of small lights hung along its roof and walls to outline its shape. In front of him was a long, narrow dock.

Crouched at the end of the dock was a dark figure.

Diggy glanced behind him. The gang was nowhere in sight.

He walked onto the dock and stopped a few yards

away from the end. The figure turned, and the lights from the boathouse lit up his face.

"So it's you," Diggy said slowly. "I might've guessed."

The other boy straightened to his full height, towering a head's-length above Diggy. It was Pete. He had finished untying a rowboat from the dock and held the end of the rope in his hand.

"I want the ring back," Diggy said, his voice steady. What was keeping the others?

"You're crazy. Do you think I'll just hand it back?" Pete said angrily.

"*You're* crazy if you think you're going to get away with this," Diggy told him.

Pete shrugged. "There are six of you and four of us. You'll say you found it, and we'll say we did. But we'll have the ring."

"Because you stole it."

"I figured it out at the same time you did," Pete said. "It's mine as much as yours. I just got there a little late, that's all. It wasn't supposed to be until three A.M."

"Was it you who dug all those holes?" Diggy asked, stalling for time.

Pete nodded. "We came out earlier today to scout around. Now, listen. I'm getting into this boat now, and I don't want you to try anything crazy. All right?" His eyes on Diggy, he moved toward the edge of the dock.

Diggy looked around; then he leaped forward and tackled him.

Pete let out an angry shout as he fell onto the dock. They wrestled, swaying near the edge. Diggy knew he couldn't hold him there for long. Pete was older, taller, and stronger. Leaning on him with one arm, Diggy dove into Pete's jacket pocket with the other hand.

Pete's right hand went instinctively to the other pocket.

Diggy grabbed Pete's hand, reached into that pocket, and pulled out the ring. He rolled away, scrambled to his feet, and began to run.

He had gone only five steps when Pete pulled him back, turned him around, and spun him down onto the dock. He grabbed the ring from Diggy's hand and ran for the boat.

He was at the edge of the dock when Diggy rolled forward and reached for one of his legs. Pete fell— and the ring flew out of his hand to fall with a *plop* into the water!

Horror-struck, both boys scrambled on their hands and knees to the side of the dock. Pete leaned forward and flailed with his hands in the current. The ring was gone.

Pete let out a howl of anger and dismay.

"You *idiot!*" he cried. With an angry shove he pushed Diggy over the edge into the river.

Diggy reached for the dock as he fell. There was a sharp *crack!* as his head hit the side of the rowboat. He felt the icy coldness of the water surrounding him. Then he passed out.

8

☐ When Diggy woke up, he was at home in bed. His mother was sitting next to him, a worried expression on her face. The members of the gang were seated around the room.

"What's going on?" Diggy asked drowsily. "What happened?"

"Never mind," his mother said. "You're going to be all right."

Diggy gazed at her blankly.

"You've had a bad bump on your head," Mrs. Caldwell explained, her voice tight. "Now, I want you to get some more sleep. You're going to be fine. And I want everyone out of this room. He needs his rest," she said, turning to the gang.

Diggy was asleep before his friends had finished filing out the door.

☐

When he opened his eyes again, Sphinx was sitting on the edge of his bed. Diggy sat up slowly and groaned. His head felt as if an express train had recently gone through it. He tried to focus his eyes.

"How do you feel?" Sphinx asked anxiously.

"Worse than I ever have in my entire life." Diggy put one hand cautiously to his head. "Oh, no."

"You had a bad fall last night. We were real worried." Sphinx shifted uncomfortably on the bed.

"I fell . . ."

"Well, you didn't exactly fall all by yourself. You had some help, remember?"

"Oh, yeah."

"We got to the dock just as Pete pushed you in. We saw the whole thing."

"What took you so long?" Diggy asked irritably. "I had to stand there trying to chat with him so he wouldn't get in the boat and leave."

"We had some problems of our own. When we got out of the woods, we were waylaid by Pete's friends. They jumped on us before we could cross the road. You got across too quickly."

"What happened?"

"Well, they were bigger, but it was five of us to three of them. And of course, we had Bobbie."

Diggy tried to focus his eyes on Sphinx. "Bobbie?"

"Uh-huh. She's been taking karate and judo in her spare time, remember? Knocking down trees and splitting blocks, things like that. She finished them off for us. They went for me and Tilo and Larry, and they were doing a pretty good job on us"—he shook his head, and Diggy noticed his swollen lip and puffy eye—"when Bobbie attacked them from behind. I've never seen anything like it. It was like watching *Revenge of the Ninja.* I've got to stop taking her to those martial arts movies."

"And Chessie?"

"She's all right. She's got a wicked kick. She says she learned it growing up in South Philly. She nearly broke one guy's leg."

"Not bad." Diggy leaned back carefully against the pillows. "So you got across the road . . ."

"Yeah, we left them there. They weren't going anywhere. We came after you and got to the dock just in time to catch Pete trying to do you in. When you hit the water, all five of us were about to go after you. But we didn't have time. It was Pete who fished you out."

"Pete?"

"Uh-huh. He went right in after you. We pulled both of you out of the water. He was scared to death. He thought he had killed you."

"And how'd you get me home?"

Sphinx looked uncomfortable. "Pete again. He had his folks' car, and he's old enough for a learner's permit. We carried you there, and he drove at about ninety miles an hour to get you to the nearest hospital. I called your parents from there."

"In the middle of the night? Oh, no."

"Yeah, your father gave us a talking-to over this whole thing that I'll never forget. I was sure they'd never let us see you again, Diggy. But the doctor said all you had was a mild concussion, and it was nothing to worry about. Pete hung around the whole time, looking scared out of his skull. Finally your folks got the okay to take you home."

"Wait a minute. What about the ring?"

Sphinx shook his head. "Gone. I hope the fish are enjoying it. It's at the bottom of the river somewhere."

Diggy groaned. "No! Say it's not true! Not after all that work and *everything!*"

"Don't tell me." Sphinx looked miserable. "Imagine how I feel."

"Oh, *damn* it!" Diggy rolled over on the bed. "What about Pete? What's going to happen to him?"

The door opened, and Diggy's mother came in. She pointed an accusing finger at Sphinx. "Out of the room, young man. *Now!*"

"Yes, ma'am, Mrs. Caldwell," Sphinx mumbled. He grinned at Diggy and grasped him by the shoulder. "I'm glad you're okay."

Diggy lay in bed, watching his mother bearing down on him. "I'm fine, Mom, really," he protested as she checked his head. "Don't fuss, *please!*"

□

"We were real worried about you," Bobbie said. She was perched on the end of his bed.

"You can say that again," Larry put in, stretching his legs out onto Diggy's desk. "I couldn't believe it when I saw Pete push you in."

Diggy leaned back on the pillows and smiled. It was Saturday afternoon, the next day, and the gang was gathered in his room. "I understand you were a real hero, Bobbie."

"Yeah, I certainly was. I *told* you that my karate and judo lessons would come in handy," she said, shooting a glance at Sphinx. "Nobody believed me."

"Not until you took on Pete's henchmen," Larry drawled. "They didn't think that you and Chessie would be much trouble before that."

"I wish they'd known better," Sphinx said. His lip was just healing. Larry had a black eye, and Tilo's cheek was cut where he had fallen against a branch.

Chessie beamed. Her pretty pointed face showed no sign of injury. Her black hair lay smoothly against her leather jacket. "It just goes to show you," she said. "Girls are better at everything."

"You won't get any argument from us," Larry said, laughing.

"So what's going to happen to Pete?" Diggy asked.

"Well," Sphinx said hesitantly, "we haven't decided yet."

"You *what?*"

"Well, he saved your life, Diggy."

"Yeah, after nearly killing me!"

"And he drove you to the hospital. The two of you were soaking wet, and we were afraid you'd get pneumonia or something out there. If we had had to wait for the bus, it would've been really bad."

"Mmm-hmm."

"Well, we didn't know what to do. Your father got

the whole story out of us, and then he called Sergeant Gauss, who came to the hospital and asked everybody lots of questions. Then he took Pete away."

"So Pete is down at the police station?"

"Oh, no. His folks came and got him. He was released into their custody. The hearing will be sometime next week."

"Okay." Diggy leaned back on the pillow, his arms crossed behind his head. "So Pete's been arrested. How about his friends?"

"He won't give their names."

"Honor among thieves, huh?" Diggy said.

"The catch, Diggy, is that we have to press charges," Chessie told him.

"So what's the problem? He stole the ring, and then he pushed me into the river."

"Yeah," said Sphinx, "but he's not such a bad guy."

"*What?*"

Sphinx looked around at the others for support. "Well, he's not," he said defensively. "You should've seen him when he thought he had hurt you."

"I couldn't. I was unconscious at the time."

"Yes, but—"

"There's another thing, Diggy," Chessie interrupted, shooting a glance at Sphinx. She leaned forward and pressed a card into Diggy's hand. "We each got one of these today."

It was an invitation, written in a thin, spidery hand in black ink on cream-colored paper. It read:

> *Mr. and Mrs. Richard J. Henning*
> *request the pleasure of your company*

at tea
on Saturday, the twenty-first of November
at four o'clock

At the bottom was *RSVP* and a Main Line address. Diggy glanced at it and then handed it back.

"There's been a big to-do in the papers," Chessie said. " 'The Dragon Ring—Lost, Found, and Lost Again,' that sort of thing. So the author herself wants to meet us. She called yesterday to find out how you were."

"Well, I'm up for meeting the Dragon Lady herself," Diggy said. "But it would've been a lot more fun making her acquaintance if we had the ring."

"You can say that again," muttered Sphinx. "Seventy-five thousand dollars!"

"Is that what the value was up to?" Diggy asked. He shook his head. "I don't believe it."

"Well, that's what the papers are saying," said Larry.

"It's a tragedy," said Sphinx darkly.

"It sure is," said Diggy.

"Do you think you'll be able to make it to the Hennings'?" asked Tilo.

"Oh, sure. I feel fine already, much better than yesterday. My mother's still standing guard over me, but I'm sure she'll lose her enthusiasm for it soon. I'll be back in school on Monday."

"Hit over the head, and all you miss is one day of school," Sphinx said. "It doesn't seem fair."

□

"So you decided to drop the charges against that other boy?" Joyce Henning said. It was Saturday afternoon, and the gang was sitting around the coffee table in her living room. There was a silver tea service on a tray next to her, and she was pouring tea and passing around silver platters piled with tiny sandwiches and tea cakes.

"That's right," Diggy replied. "We thought about it a long time and then decided that since the ring was lost anyway, pressing charges against him wouldn't bring it back. And apparently Pete never meant to push me into the river, although you could have fooled me at the time. He was the one who fished me out."

Joyce Henning nodded. She was a stately-looking woman in her early sixties, with beautifully cut silver hair. "The papers have been full of nothing else. It's the curiosity of the season." She turned to her husband. "I knew we'd make news, Richard, but not this way."

Richard Henning was a short man with white hair and gray eyes. "We were shocked to hear about it, to put it mildly," he said. "We had planned to give the ring away and were waiting to see who would find it, but we never in our wildest dreams thought the Schuylkill River would inherit our heirloom." He motioned to Sphinx to pass one of the platters. Sphinx had it on his lap and was absentmindedly eating one cookie after another.

The gang had been taken aback by the splendor of

the Hennings' home. The house could not be seen from the street; only a stone gate with the name of the house, *Eversley,* was visible. The driveway curved through a row of trees, with a manicured lawn sloping away on either side. The building itself was an English-style country home with half-timbered walls and leaded windows. There was a stained-glass rose set in one of the living room windows that, Mrs. Henning had told them, had been imported from England at her mother-in-law's request: it had originally been part of a country house owned by Elizabeth I. Other parts of the house had been imported from England as well: floor tiles, stained glass windows, wooden beams, entire walls. "My mother-in-law very much wanted a home in England," Mrs. Henning said, smiling, "but since she couldn't have that, she did the next best thing: She had bits and pieces of country houses, as they became available, shipped over here and reassembled. The result is this house, a total hodgepodge."

Mr. Henning shook his head. "My wife has never gotten used to it."

"It's just like a real English country house: hot in the summer and cold in the winter," his wife said with a sniff.

"But I love it," Mr. Henning continued. "I would never live anywhere else."

"Fortunately we had modern plumbing installed, so the place is livable," Mrs. Henning added. "But only just."

"I'd say it's more than livable," Chessie remarked.

The others agreed. The late afternoon sun poured in the windows. The rugs on the floor glowed softly, red and blue and gold. There were old paintings on the walls and antique furniture, inlaid writing desks, spindly wooden chairs, and silk sofas.

"Oh, well, it's all right," Joyce Henning said grudgingly. "But that's enough about the house, Richard. I invited you here, all of you, to express our condolences about the loss of the ring. We were terribly sorry to hear about it. And, well, Richard and I came up with an idea. We don't want you to walk away empty-handed from our treasure hunt. We know how long and hard you worked on it. I may have told the newspapers that the clues were easy if you looked at them the right way"—she smiled—"but that's always true for the person who happened to make them up. I know some of them must have been very difficult to crack."

"You can say that again," Sphinx said with some heat.

"We want to let you know that we appreciate your following it all the way through," she said.

The gang glanced at each other. *Money,* Sphinx thought, *I smell money.*

"So we want you to have these." Mrs. Henning went over to her writing desk and opened a side drawer. She pulled out six blue envelopes. "It's not much—not what you would have gotten for the ring, I'm afraid—but it's a sign of our appreciation of your talent and perseverance." She handed the stack of envelopes to Diggy.

"We can't make up for the ring," Mr. Henning said, leaning back on the sofa and putting his arm around his wife, "but we wanted to do what we could to make you feel better."

Each envelope had a name written on it in gold ink.

"An affectation," Mrs. Henning said apologetically. "My gold ink. Everyone hates it but me."

"Thank you very much, Mr. and Mrs. Henning," Diggy said. "We really do appreciate it." He made no move to open the envelopes.

The others were staring at him. Sphinx was nearly frothing at the mouth with eagerness. Diggy gave them all a hard stare and jerked his head slightly toward the Hennings.

"Uh—yes," Bobbie said, recovering. "Thanks so much for, ummm, whatever it is. It's very kind of you."

"Thank you," Chessie chimed in, raising her cup of tea and taking a sip to hide her confusion. "Thanks very much."

The other three, caught off guard, mumbled their thanks. Sphinx gulped and reached for a handful of cookies.

"Why, Richard, look," said Mrs. Henning with a smile, putting a hand on her husband's arm. "What well-mannered children. I've never seen anything like it. If only our own children had been as beautifully raised."

"Amazing," her husband acknowledged. "It's astonishing."

"Please open them, all of you," she said. "The suspense is killing me."

"Are you sure?" Diggy asked, his hand wavering over the pile of envelopes.

"She's sure!" Sphinx cried. He grabbed the top one. "This one's for you, Tilo." Tilo sat looking at it as if afraid to open it. "Here's mine," Sphinx said. He ripped it open. "Why—why, thanks!" He sounded genuinely surprised.

Chessie opened hers. Inside was a check for a thousand dollars. She gulped and looked up at the Hennings. "Ummm—thanks so much, but that's really too much money," she said. "I'm not sure we should take it."

"Don't give me your scruples," Sphinx groaned. "Just thank them nicely, okay?"

"It's all right," Mrs. Henning said, laughing. "We've made enough on the book to cover that and more. It's nothing, Chessie, don't worry about it. Invest it for your future. Richard is very good at things like that. He's an investment banker. He can advise you."

The thanks came in a rush from the six of them. The afternoon passed pleasantly. At six o'clock Diggy glanced at his watch and stood up.

"It's been a real pleasure," he said. "Thanks so much for the tea and the gifts and everything."

"I'm glad that you're up and around again," Mrs. Henning replied. "Don't get into any more scrapes, all right, Diggy?"

"Don't worry. I swear I'm not doing anything but

schoolwork for a while. We have to catch up after all the time we spent working on your clues."

"It warms an old professor's heart to hear you talk about homework," Mrs. Henning said, rising to her feet. "Come, I'll walk everyone to the door."

They shook hands with her and left. Her husband drove them into town. At Diggy's door he waved off their thanks and wished them luck for the future. "I have a feeling we'll be hearing about the six of you again someday," he said with a laugh. "It seems to me you're not the type to keep quiet for long."

"Oh, yes we are," Diggy said fervently. "For a while, anyway."

As Mr. Henning drove off Sphinx said, "Nice guy."

"Nice gifts," said Larry.

"Wow," Chessie said, pulling the envelope out of her pocket. "I'm going home to spend the evening looking at this. Coming, Tilo?" They set off together.

Bobbie lingered for a moment. "It's Saturday night," she said. "Anybody interested in a movie?"

Diggy shook his head. "My head still hurts," he said. "I'm going to sleep early."

Sphinx wavered a moment, then said, "Oh, wait, I forgot. My folks are having friends over for the evening, and I'm supposed to dance attendance. You guys are invited if you want," he said to Bobbie and Larry.

Bobbie made a face. "Never mind. Another time." She and Larry waved good-bye.

"How are you feeling?" Sphinx asked Diggy.

"Not too bad. But I'm going to take it easy for the rest of the evening," Diggy said.

□

At ten o'clock that night the phone rang. Diggy leaned over the sofa to pick it up. "Hello?"

"Diggy? Sphinx. Listen. I know you're not feeling well, so you won't be too happy about this right away, but I just know you'll love it once you think it over. I was reading today's paper—"

"What happened to your guests?"

Sphinx sounded disgusted. "They're playing bridge. How can people play that game? It's so boring, except when you fight with your partner. Listen to this. I was just reading the paper when I came across this article." Diggy could hear the sound of pages rustling. "Marathon Relay Race," read Sphinx. "Ages ten to fourteen. Distance: sixty miles. Number of contestants per relay: six. *Six*, okay? This thing has our names written all over it. The race will take place in March—we can start training now—and goes all around the city in a loop through Fairmount Park, ending with a run down the Benjamin Franklin Parkway. It begins and ends at the art museum, just like *Rocky*. You run up the steps of the art museum at the end—that is, I mean, if you make it that far. Now listen: 'First prize is three thousand dollars,' *three thousand dollars*, Diggy, 'second prize is fifteen hundred dollars, and third prize is six hundred dollars.' But I'm positive we'll win first prize. Bobbie can run real well, and I'm not so bad, and Tilo's real fast too, and the rest of you, well, you can learn. We'll train real hard starting now. I can't wait! It's going to be *great!*"

A grin spread slowly over Diggy's tired face. "Sphinx?"

"Yeah?"

"Good night." With a click he hung up the phone.

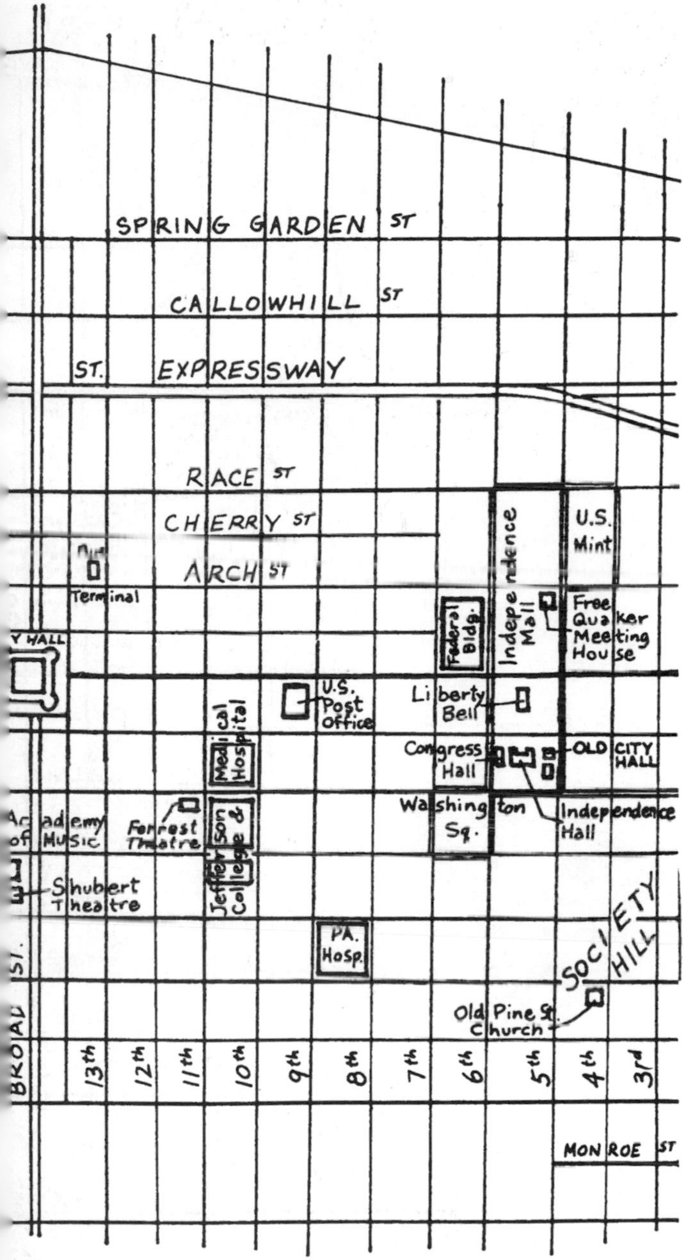
SPRING GARDEN ST
CALLOWHILL ST
ST. EXPRESSWAY
RACE ST
CHERRY ST
ARCH ST
Terminal
Y HALL
U.S. Mint
Independence Mall
Federal Bldg.
Free Quaker Meeting House
U.S. Post Office
Liberty Bell
Medical Hospital
Congress Hall
OLD CITY HALL
Academy of Music
Forrest Theatre
Jefferson College
Washington Sq.
Independence Hall
Shubert Theatre
PA. Hosp.
SOCIETY HILL
Old Pine St. Church
BROAD ST.
13th
12th
11th
10th
9th
8th
7th
6th
5th
4th
3rd
MONROE ST

ABOUT THE AUTHORS

MILTON DANK grew up in Philadelphia, attended the University of Pennsylvania, from which he holds a doctorate in physics, and has worked as a research physicist in the aerospace industry.

Mr. Dank has written several novels for young adult readers, including *The Dangerous Game, Game's End, Khaki Wings,* and *Red Flight Two. The Computer Caper, A UFO Has Landed,* and *The 3-D Traitor,* written in collaboration with his daughter, Gloria, are the first three books in the Galaxy Gang Mystery series.

GLORIA DANK graduated from Princeton University with a bachelor's degree in psychology and has worked as a computer analyst. She is currently working on her second fantasy novel.

Milton Dank and Gloria Dank live and work in suburban Philadelphia.